Cacophony of Crowns

OF CROWNS

Garrett S. Broussard

To Libby, for endless support, nurturing, and compassion through the hardest of times. Thank you for loving me exactly as I am and exactly as I want to be.

To my baby Dunny Bunny, the floofster. May you live forever in the hearts and memories of those you loved while you chase all the squirrels you can find wherever you are. I miss you, buddy.

To my Mom, for being my original #1 fan and almost getting kicked out of a movie theater for trying to take a picture of my first credit. I hope you have found peace and forgiveness in your new eternity.

To anyone out there with stories in their heads, it's time to share them and take your crown.

Contents

A Book is a Book   1

Book One
  Dark Forest   5
    Outsider   5
    Guardian   10
    Student   17
  Among the Trees   25
  Ascension   26
    Vengeance   26
    Turmoil   31
  Trespassers   37
  Green Hood   49
  A Meaningful Obsession   60
  Grab the Booty   61
  Vampyr Killer   65
  Atansha   69
    Coronation   69
    Rebellion   73
  General of the Winds   78
    Diplomacy   78
  Born of Flame   85
    Saboteur   85
  Sea Witch   94
    Psychopomp   94
  Shy Not   100
  Celestial Mother   101
  Chthonic Father   104
    Fear   104

Book Two
   Binky   113
   Embrace the Change   120
   Lemonberry   134
   My Heart Hurts   135

Book Three
   The Bar Dive   141
   Reverbs vs Juicers   148
   Acknowledgments
   About the Author

Disclaimer

If you haven't questioned your existence before now, I urge you to reconsider before proceeding.

A Book is a Book

A book is a book, even when it is banned,

For the pages are bound and the leather is tanned.

So seek not permission from those who surround you,

For their goodness and morals surely will drown you.

Ignore their shrill voices, you cannot be bothered,

For their aim is control, to see curiosity smothered.

So pick up a pen, a paper or pad,

Tell the world your story, the life that you've had.

And listen to others whose voices are stifled,

For they are more than just words, more than mere trifles.

Let's open our minds, and give in to learning,

And stop all this fuckery, and the needless burning.

Book One

The Past

A look back in time as it was.
A time filled with kings and queens, swords and sorcery,
magick and powerful deities.

Dark Forest

Outsider

Under the shade of an old tangled oak tree kneels a man covered shoulder-to-toe in what was once brilliantly shining armor. The tree lies just outside an old-growth forest with a canopy so dense that little to no light reaches the undergrowth. The forest's edge has an uncanny silence about it and a complete lack of animals, save for a few curious fox-like creatures with multiple tails and an unbelievable ability to navigate the dense vegetation.

The forest spans for miles on either side with only one gap, a large circular clearing where a wide path ends abruptly at the treeline. In the other direction, the path leads over the river, across the valley, and up into the snowy mountains that sit like teeth biting into the blue sky above. The path winds freely for hundreds of miles, but isn't bold enough to enter this forest without permission—a feat accidentally attempted by the broken man near the tree.

The kneeling man's helmet lies on the ground supporting an arm weary from travel and battle while the other arm provides comfort to his pained insides. His pale and jaundiced face is covered in dirt, blood, and a beard so long and unkempt that it carries small pieces of the plants he's encountered on his journey—and even pieces of a few animals. Even though his armor is battered, the damage is too recent to have rusted the skillfully forged steel.

The exhausted warrior shows no sign of aggression and is swarmed by small radiant firebugs native to the nearby forest. The bugs give off a glow of verdigris like a rich green forest filtered through the morning fog, a telltale sign of the magick flowing through them.

At the boundary of the forest, for which this ancient tree is an ambassador and a greeter, stands a troupe of forest-dwelling humans guarding their home from high in the canopy. Two archers, with arrows drawn, flank a third man in an elegant robe who surveys the newcomer. The robed leader's dark hair peeks out over the ochre skin of his forehead, as if it too is curious about the situation.

A blue-green campfire burns on a nearby branch to provide warmth, but the self-fueled flames pose no risk to the tree. Curled up next to the campfire are two more vulpine animals, known to the locals as kitrits. The larger kitrit boasts tails that are a brilliant mix of reds, oranges, and browns as fiery as the magick within it. Its neighbor has a tan body with brown and green tails covered in vibrant flowers and moss.

"Shall I fire, sir?" The younger archer asks his leader, Kanim.

"No, but keep your bows drawn," says Kanim. "We'll leave the outsider's fate to the Guardian."

Dark Forest

Kanim fetches a wooden whistle flute from his side and begins to play an inaudible melody for an unseen audience. The mouthpiece of the whistle is carved into the shape of a mythical wolf-like animal and covered in runes of an ancient language. Hand-carved finger holes pass in and out of sight as his hands form the notes of his song. The melody passes furtively through the trees, beyond the village, and well into the darkest depths of the forest. No response is given, but the leader seems pleased with the result.

The second archer, a short man with a deep scowl on his pinkish face, fires an arrow that strikes the ground just in front of the outsider, causing a small panic in the weary man.

The leader, Kanim, turns towards the archer and asks, "Why did you shoot at our guest?"

"Consider it a conversation starter," he sneers. "Now he knows we're watching."

"Let me do the talking from now on, then. Our rules exist for a reason." Kanim lowers the archer's bow and pats him on the back as he nimbly makes his way down from the outpost in the canopy and heads into the village. The path to the village is overgrown in places, but the locals know to follow the line of connected tree roots sticking just above the dirt. His walk through the forest is plagued by fears of the unseen eyes watching him from the trees, but he continues on as he has for years. Kanim walks for just over an hour through dense ferns and grasses before arriving at a massive clearing that marks the entrance to the arboreal village.

The village feels both ethereal and primitive, with roaring

blue-green fires that provide warmth and much needed light to the space and odd-shaped trees that house the villagers. These old and intricate structures were formed by sorcerers of the village who were allowed to guide the growth of the trees in exchange for protecting the forest from outside harm—a reciprocal relationship unknown elsewhere in the world.

The ever-growing branches of the ancient trees twist and turn to form the roofs, doors, and walls that hold their inhabitants. Some branches of neighboring trees have melded together to form pathways between them. Mosses and ferns soften the branches comprising the flooring and provide comfortable bedding as well. Each dwelling has complete privacy thanks to smaller trees that have taken root in the freshly formed dirt and partially decayed vegetation wedged into the elbows of larger, older trees high above the forest floor.

Down at ground level, the village children climb on rocks and low lying branches to play with their pet kitrits, and the array of beautifully colored animals pops against the verdant backdrop. Children squeal joyfully as they chase their canine friends and pet their many fluffy tails. The kitrits enjoy the attention and the bone-in meat given to them by the parents in exchange for babysitting.

Meanwhile, the adults drink and dance around the fires while enchanted instruments fill the evening air with music. Stringed instruments, both bowed and plucked, as well as flutes and pipes dance along with the humans. Hand drums and other percussion instruments are played by sticks and rocks moved by unseen hands to provide the beat. The music is primal and calming, the perfect accompaniment to the songs of the residents. The songs thank the forest for what it's provided and ask it to continue providing for them through the next season.

The innermost circle of ritual leaders wear animal hides over their heads and shoulders, with a varied amount of clothes worn underneath. They dance in unison around the flames while chanting and singing together. One woman in the circle, a smaller woman with tawny skin and a large deer hide worn in lieu of clothes, makes eye contact with Kanim and breaks from the circle. She races over to him and places her soft skin against his body while covering him in loving kisses.

"It's feast night, darling." Her drunken words still retain an air of intelligence amidst the undertones of lust and laughter. "Please come dance, the forest will be fine tonight!"

"I can't, Dinestra. We're holding an outsider on the edge of the forest. A battered man in an expensive suit of armor." His words send a sobering shock through her entire body while he weighs his need to protect the village against his urge to join her under her deer hide, as is tradition after a feast.

"Do you trust him? Do we bring him in? Is he hungry?" Her mouth doesn't stop moving but her words trail off into a private internal monologue.

"We do nothing. I've called for the Guardian and I'm only here to gather enough supplies to last until he arrives."

"Has he responded?" Dinestra asks with a gasp.

"No response," he says with an air of frustration. "I used the whistle just as he showed me."

"Shhh," she interrupts. "I know you did it right, Kanim. Do

it again, make sure he knows you're serious. You know as well as I do that those magickal types wait to help us until situations are truly dire. We'll miss you at the feast, but there will always be another."

Kanim nods and blows the whistle again before returning to where he left the outsider, leaving Dinestra to rejoin the ritual circle. He draws slow, careful breaths and pays close attention to every inaudible note he plays. The repeated melody travels further into the forest, landing on the only pair of human ears to hear the sound. Those ears belong to a man with a long, reddish-gray beard sitting next to a magickal alpine lake miles from the sound's origin.

Guardian

The lake glows with the signature glacial blue hue of nature magick and is deep enough to house primordial creatures that sometimes swim up from the unknown depths of the planet.

The man's face is adorned with both youth and wisdom, a balance not uncommon among the truly gifted magick users of the world. His skin is a pale pink with a hint of fawn, like snow reflecting the evening sunlight. His eyes, gray and speckled like the craters of the moon, hold the wisdom of his years spent in the service of magick. His body and head are covered in a hooded robe made of thick green material, and in his lap sits a black and brown dog with tired amber eyes that sighs and drifts off to sleep.

Next to the bearded sorcerer sits a celestial woman who kicks her bare, porcelain feet in the lake, sending out waves of starlight in all manner of hues and textures. The starlight provides magick to the lake, which feeds the rivers that flow through the entire forest, thus providing the main source of magick for the region. Her long silver hair drapes over her glowing gown as she twirls the end of one strand with her delicate fingers. The pair sit by the lake as they have for centuries, playing, laughing, and caring for their pets—both living critters and spectral beings conjured by the woman.

The man's ears perk up as the melody reaches him, and he makes eye contact with his lover to signal his inevitable departure.

"Go where you're needed, Elstaer," she says while gently sliding the dog off the man's lap. "We'll be here when you get back."

Elstaer grabs a wooden staff from the ground behind him before darting towards the forest entrance. He runs along the lake shore to a path leading down the mountain to the village. He propels himself forward with his staff and leaps off a small cliff as he shifts his body into that of a massive wolf-like creature with multiple reddish tails and a large mane. His face is much more stern than that of the kitrits, and his shoulders are easily taller than an average sized human. He lets out a loud howl in response to Kanim's melody.

Elstaer picks up speed instantly, bounding between

branches and the rocky terrain below. He passes by the same unseen eyes that terrified Kanim earlier, but pays no attention to them. Even hungry predators have limits, and every animal in the forest knows of Elstaer's power—though some are still willing to challenge him. The darkness dissipates as he nears the edge of the forest, and he picks up even more speed before bursting out from behind the trees.

Elstaer, the Guardian, approaches the newcomer still in his beast form, running directly up to him. He circles the downed knight, breathing heavily and sniffing him to detect signs of foul magick. The knight avoids eye contact to show his resignation but manages to hide his shaking so that only he and the firebugs inside his armor notice it. The Guardian takes note of the number of fireflies surrounding the man and eases up on his interrogation slightly.

"Why have you come to my forest?" Elstaer growls through his sharp teeth and stands between the man and the forest entrance.

"I was told the forest is capable of great healing, something I require."

"Yes," says Elstaer. "It is *capable* of it. Though I find the forest to be picky about who it *chooses* to heal. Tell me, who put this fantasy in your head? Did he have ulterior motives when sending you here?"

"I don't know her name, or even what she truly looks like. In every encounter she bore a new body, but still had that same melodic voice, and the smell of fresh flowers consumed me while in her presence."

Elstaer pauses and tilts his canine head out of curiosity. "Did *she* now? And what did this mystery woman say to you? What did she *do* to compel you to risk your life by coming here? Clearly, this journey was nearly too much for you to handle."

"I've come from Selanor up in the mountains, where I served as a knight for the royal army. My family has fallen into destitution and fighting was the only way I could earn money. My father hated my choice and wanted me to stay as his errand boy for the inn, but I couldn't take it. I'm good at fighting and was able to climb the ranks easily—success is a rare occurrence among the Omnarrup family. I've come here because I began to question what I was fighting for, because of that mystery woman."

"As for the woman, I first saw her back in Selanor when our troops were marching off to battle. She stood outside a flower shop in a white dress and I swear her presence caused the flowers around her to bloom. She said nothing, but the look on her face made me question the war for the first time in my life."

"Next, I saw her on the battlefield among the warring soldiers, seemingly invisible to everyone but me. This time she wore an ethereal green dress and a crown when she asked me if this was the life I wanted. She turned my gaze to the carnage around me, and I couldn't bring myself to tell her that I agreed with the war."

Elstaer continues nodding when a flash of light catches the corner of his eye. He looks over to see a tall and powerful woman in a green dress far away behind a tree. She holds back a tear in her eye and gives him a pleading look. Elstaer notices a vine growing from the oak tree that seems to caress the broken soldier's back lovingly. He nods at the woman and turns back into his robed human form, much to the shock of the soldier, but urges the man to continue his story.

"I followed her off the battlefield, where she disappeared and left behind a ball of blue light like those around me now. As I approached the light it jumped miles away to the edge of my vision, tempting me to follow. This continued for months, leading me through villages, over mountain ranges, and across vast prairies until I met her again in the meadow beyond the river behind me."

"She bore another body in a flowing purple dress, dancing in the field among the blooming flowers. The winds were strong that day, but I saw her move the field like the waves of the ocean. Her song echoed through the valley and her dance shook the earth around her. When she noticed me I felt the earth move and sway around me, then the flowers turned liquid and I began to float in them. The ocean of grass and flowers healed my most dire physical wounds and I heard her voice singing to me, telling me to enter this forest in search of what I needed. She told me that what I seek is among the trees, which I knew to be the healing I mentioned to you."

"Baffling," Elstaer mutters to himself as he picks up the man's head to get a better look at his tired face. "For Atansha to take an interest in *you*, I never would have imagined it."

Elstaer continues his long stare in the direction where the woman was, and signals to the troupe of guards to bring the injured man into the forest. The newcomer is confused by Elstaer's apparent knowledge of the woman, and his refusal to share the information, but is much too weak to protest.

"This fool needs healing, likely more than he realizes. See to his hunger, and I shall return to check on him after some time." He doesn't break concentration as the man is carried away to the village.

"Welcome to the Dark Forest, young Omnarrup. I hope you're brave enough to explore its darkest depths." Elstaer lets out a confused chuckle, then decides to share the news with his family up by the lake. His excitement is contagious, but he knows to hide it from the humans who don't understand what has been set in motion.

Elstaer returns to his home at the alpine lake and informs his lover about the outsider. She kicks her feet out of the water and jumps up immediately.

"Really?! Could it really be him? I want to see him! Let's go babies, we're on a mission." Starglow drips from the woman as she stands and gathers their pets for the journey.

"Rowan," says Elstaer, trying to hide his hesitation. "I'll lead, but look at him from afar, please."

"Elstaer," says Rowan casually, "I taught you everything you know."

Rowan performs a small ritual to gather starglow around her and forms it into a large cat-like creature for the long journey. She hops on its back and takes some of the smaller critters with her, brimming with excitement, as they head towards the village.

The pack arrives at the village a few hours later, and Elstaer enters the healing hut to check on the newcomer. The man lays unconscious on a bed grown from the branches of the tree that forms the walls. His body is covered in vines and flowers, with the densest areas tending to his worst wounds. Kanim and the village elders stand around the bed, chanting to aid in his recovery.

"How is he doing?" Asks Elstaer.

"Some of his wounds go deep, but he has an incredible will to survive," says one of the elders. She is clothed in a dark cloak that covers her old body and her face is wrinkled from age, but has a softness to it. Her cloak is fastened with vines as an homage to her patron goddess.

"Good to hear," says Elstaer. "Thank you for tending to our unexpected guest, I know Atansha will appreciate it as well." The elderly woman's smile grows at the thought of pleasing her goddess.

Elstaer takes a moment to survey the newcomer. He looks over the knight's broken armor on the ground next to him, looking for sigils that may confirm his suspicions. The pauldron that once protected the knight's left shoulder bears a sigil of a beam of light descending into a barren valley.

Elstaer leaves the hut to share the news with Rowan, who is playing with her hair and petting the large glowing beast she rode to the village.

"It's him. He bears the symbol of the light," says Elstaer.

"Strange," she says. "His line has definitely lessened with the years. I remember them being taller, and bloodier."

"Not all humans master the magickal arts," says Elstaer.

"This one just might, but he has a way to go. That's enough excitement for one day, I'm going back home." She kisses Elstaer's cheek and sets off with the pack in tow. Elstaer smiles as he watches his family walk away, then leaves to meet with the village elders again to continue planning their guest's rehabilitation.

Student

The outsider awakens a week later in the healing hut, weary and confused. He basks in the intricate natural architecture and the collection of odd trinkets spread throughout the room. He hears faint footsteps as the Guardian of the Forest enters.

"You're awake," says Elstaer. "Your strength is returning quickly. I see you've cleaned up a bit and the warmth has returned to your face."

"Yes, the beard is new, though I prefer it shorter and more manageable as it is now. Not that yours looks bad! Thanks... Thank you for taking me in and healing me."

"Thank the forest, it *chose* to heal you." Elstaer shows a small smile.

"I hear them call you Elstaer, that's a unique name. I noticed you haven't asked about mine, aren't you curious who I am?"

"I'm indeed curious, but your name doesn't answer that

question. I'm interested in what brought you here, and why she chose you. Tell me, where do your passions lie?"

"This woman, you seem to know her. Who is she and what does she want with me?"

"You know what she wants you to know." Elstaer motions for the outsider to answer his question regardless of his lack of a helpful answer in return.

"I am a knight who enjoys forging weapons between battles." The outsider squirms with discomfort as he finishes his sentence.

"I trust you see that your former title cannot be regained any easier than you can regain the past and the latter hobby serves you no longer here in this village. Do your creations extend beyond war implements?"

"I," the outsider hesitates to finish his sentence, "I sometimes make jewelry for my loved ones."

"Wonderful. I'm eager to see what you're capable of."

The outsider looks around at the wooden house and questions how he can smith anything metal, let alone something as delicate as jewelry, in a place like this.

"I would need a forge and rare metals for that..."

Elstaer returns a blank stare at the still-wounded man while puffing on a long pipe that emits a smell both sweet and earthy.

"Correct. Luckily for you, the villagers craft many metal things and the forest is full of rare metals and gemstones. I trust you'll find everything you need here, provided you know where to look." His words end with a coy smile.

"And what if I choose to leave here after I'm healed?"

"Then you'll be gone," says Elstaer plainly. "You will be healed, and owe nothing to the forest or its inhabitants."

The outsider relaxes upon discovering that he is truly a guest, not a prisoner.

"I should warn you, though," says Elstaer. "We both know you came here searching for a way to heal more than just your body. Your elusive friend led you here, yet you followed her for a reason you can't quite explain. An honorable knight left an active battlefield to follow a strange woman to a dark forest where he makes jewelry and speaks in riddles with a wise old shapeshifter. Yet you are happy here, you've felt it since you feared for your life under the tree. You'll never find out why you did these things, or why you *feel* these things, and that void will grow and grow until it consumes you entirely. You've tasted contentment, and that hunger will never subside nor will it be satiated outside this forest."

Elstaer pauses, then begins to leave the hut and says, "But at least you'll be back home where you feel safe, right?" He shoots the newcomer a wink and gives him a firm pat on the back on his way out.

⊕ ⊕ ⊕

Two months pass as the outsider tries his luck at his new hobby. Most of his creations are failures and are melted down to use for his next attempt. He manages a few pieces that are successful, but his progress is slow.

The outsider walks up to a young man about his age, a

shorter man with a long black jacket and a crisp white shirt. A well detailed knife sticks out from his jacket, fastened by a leather belt. The knife has a translucent white handle covered in gold filigree that extends to the polished steel blade next to it.

"I like your knife," says the outsider. "I can teach you how to make a knife like that."

"Thank you, but I made this one myself. We all learn to make weapons before advancing to jewelry. You'll learn it too, if you keep trying." The smith's face cracks like hot steel as he smiles.

The outsider feigns a smile back and asks, "When did you learn to make jewelry? It seems natural to you."

"I was only a boy when I became an apprentice. I don't remember a time before I knew the trade, honestly."

"Your tools just don't make sense to me." The outsider hears a low growl from behind the trees and shuffling in the underbrush. "Did you hear that? It sounds like something is out there."

"That's because there *is* something out there. Terrible predators live just beyond our village, that's why I never leave."

"That sounds like the woods near where I used to play as a boy. Dangerous things in those trees." His eyes glaze over and a single droplet falls from his face as he thinks back to his childhood. His momentary lapse causes his hammer to fall with the weight of ten strikes onto a necklace he's spent two weeks making, shattering it instantly. He lets out a shout and storms into his hut, where he finds Elstaer waiting.

"Not now," says the angry blacksmith apprentice.

"Sit down," Elstaer responds cooly and firmly.

"I'm angry, wolf man. Not now."

"So be angry," Elstaer says as he motions to a chair. "Angry and seated."

"Are you familiar with the story of Meersh?" Elstaer asks in an abrupt subject change.

"Not very. No. I believe he's looked upon as a heretic by some in my city and a myth by the rest."

"He was a brave man and a great storyteller. Most of all, he was the fastest being to ever walk this earth. So fast that he could run around the world in a matter of seconds. One day, he ran so fast that he lifted off the ground and ran into the sky. Most believe he died that day, drifting among the stars for an eternity. I, however, got to meet him thousands of years later after he returned from his voyage. He told stories of the other planets and incredible beings he passed on his journey. I believe he is still out there, living out eternity with another species of beings. Some say that he has taken others out among the stars to a place of their choosing to start new worlds of their own."

"I can't say I believe what I'm hearing, Elstaer. Where do I fit into this story?"

"Right where you are, as always. You see," says Elstaer, "Meersh ended up somewhere he never intended to be, but he followed his curiosity and explored the cosmos. No one remembers what he did before his voyage, but he left behind an inspiring legacy—among the well-educated, that is."

Elstaer's words strike a chord with the newcomer, causing him to fixate on his struggle with inexperience at the craft of jewelry making rather than the anger raging inside him.

"I'm not cut out for making jewelry like this, everything I touch is ruined."

"I'm always amazed by the impatience of mortals, expecting everything to happen on their short timeline. Your teachers weren't born with their skills. It's an odd thing, making jewelry. The material is dense and hardly malleable, every cut on the stone tells the story of its creation, and every swing of the hammer has to be precise. Yet every piece is also delicate and requires care. A sword can be hammered until it's flat enough to take a life and it's considered finished. A piece of jewelry, however, is a piece of art. Stop trying to finish the necklace and experience yourself making it."

"You seem to know a lot about smithing. Why are you helping me?" The newcomer asks.

"I told your friend I would, and the bread is better down here in the village." Elstaer takes a large bite out of a fresh roll.

"I'm just surprised a god like you would spend his time on me. Do you treat all your visitors this well?"

Elstaer chuckles with a mouth full of bread, tears off an untouched piece, and tosses it to his new friend.

"We haven't had a visitor in a few centuries, since the forest was much smaller than it is now. No, I'm no god, though I have managed to bend the rules governing the mortal plane to my advantage. True gods can control the primordial spirits of the world, like the man who is able to boil the earth itself by controlling both earth and fire. Or the Lord of Storms who controls air and water to conjure storms great enough to level entire cities. Think of your friend, who can summon new life around her and control this very forest. No, I still bow to the earth spirits but the gods have found a way to flip that relationship."

"So she was mortal once?"

"Yes, her and the other gods."

"Why haven't you ascended to the level of god?" His curiosity brings on a flippant tone that shocks them both.

"All power has its price, young student. Some of the gods have found that out for themselves. I have no interest in paying that price."

"But who can punish a god if they have control over the spirits? Surely that would take an incomprehensible amount of power."

"There are those who have never known mortality, ones that have existed since the beginning of time. The ones who influence our actions in their quests for power. That's a talk for a different day, it's probably best you learn how to make a necklace before you attempt to comprehend the entirety of existence."

Elstaer hands the newcomer a book about smithing which bears sigils very similar to ones carved into Elstaer's staff. The book feels ancient and is full of detailed knowledge about working with different metals and gemstones.

"Read up," Elstaer says. "You have much to learn and I'll be gone for a few weeks. Try to walk through the forest between your lessons, you'll learn even more out there than you'd expect."

Elstaer leaves the hut and the newcomer thumbs through page after page of knowledge. A sense of relief comes over him as he processes the words of the Guardian, yet he knows he has much to learn before mastering his new craft.

Among the Trees

Should you find yourself on the edge of a forest,

Wondering whether to heed the call to enter,

Know that the voice you hear is your own and that desire burns within.

Know that the questions that arise while you stare into the darkness

Need not stay unanswered forever.

Know that what you seek is among the trees.

Ascension

Vengeance

On the outskirts of a small and sparse forest, a young girl plays with her imaginary friends. She jumps around and giggles as she rides on the back of a magickal beast, then waves at a man walking towards her to signal him to climb on the beast. The man ignores her invitation and fiddles with a small dagger in his belt as he continues towards her.

"Well hello, little girl," he says with an evil smile. "Is your father about? I'm a messenger with some questions for him."

"Nope," says the little girl while shaking her head, completely unaware of the dangerous situation.

"Alright then. I'll leave the message with you instead," says the man as he lunges towards her and draws his dagger.

Crack! The assassin is frozen solid by a spell cast from the other side of the clearing. Three men run up to the little girl frantically, one of whom holds her tightly in his arms and checks her for injuries.

"Are you ok?! Where is Namira?" The father is muscular, with soft facial features, pinkish skin, and dark hair.

"I'm ok, she went to fetch more water for mommy. Why is

that man frozen?"

"It's a fun game we're playing, sweetie. He has a weird laugh so don't mind any noises you hear from the forest later."

"I'm here! I'm so sorry, Mr. Erphin," says a woman between deep exhausted breaths as she runs to join the group.

"Yes, you are, Namira. Take her to her mother, please. And fetch the Surgeon. Tell her to meet us in the chamber with her tools and her imagination." Erphin shoots a look at Namira that makes her blood run cold then smiles at his daughter and waves goodbye to her.

"Nice shot, Plyntys," says Erphin. "You two get him to the chamber before he thaws. I'm curious what other messages he has for me." He signals the other two to drag the ice block off into the woods while he follows close behind.

The trio arrives at an old tree stump deep in the woods, far beyond the reach of the sun. Erphin opens a cellar door attached to the stump and holds it open as Plyntys and his cohort drag the frozen man into the chamber. The subterranean dwelling is formed by stones propped up between the thick roots of the tree above, and the floor below is mostly dirt and mulch with an occasional stone that hasn't yet been covered. In the middle of the space lies a stone table large enough to hold a human for medical operations, or torture in this case, which is a similar procedure performed with a vastly different intent.

A tall and skinny woman with obsidian skin and salt and pepper curls wearing a leather apron over a clean white shirt stands at the table prepping her tools. The look on the Surgeon's face is determined and mildly excited as she rolls out the restraints. She gestures for the men to place the prisoner on the table and Erphin casts a fiery spell to melt the remaining ice, not at all cautious to avoid burning the prisoner who attempted to murder his daughter. He shakes his hand in pain after the spell—fire magick has a great cost when performed by a novice.

"Be careful, Erphin. These woods feed off any evil we allow to grow inside us," says Plyntys with a shaky voice while looking around the room fearfully. The others ignore his concerns and the roots of the tree wiggle as if caught in a breeze as thoughts of terrible deeds grow in their minds.

Plyntys vacates the chamber to avoid the dastardly sight, but the thin walls aren't enough to shield his ears from the shrieks caused by the Surgeon's skillful deeds. He eventually hears something about the village who hired the assassin.

"I fucking knew it," says Erphin. "It's been years of their attacks and now they went after what little family I have left! Tell the others I've gone hunting to clear my thoughts and dispose of what's left of this assassin."

The angry father storms out of the chamber in search of a horse, and Plyntys follows closely after him. The lie about hunting is not entirely false, vanquishing the entire village would ease his thoughts and a hunt is about to happen.

"Stay home, Plyntys. This won't be any easier to stomach than what our good Surgeon has done." Plyntys completely ignores him and continues to procure horses for the journey. As they ride past the rival village, Plyntys opens his mouth to comment but only musters a silent protest. They ride up to a tall mountain bare of trees, snow, and other life forms. Its stone cliffs are scorched by years of fires and the burn trails all lead to a single cave halfway up to the summit.

"The mountain, but, but that's where..." stutters Plyntys out of sheer terror.

Up the mountain and into the cave they go, so dark, so silent, so much gold. The walls of the cave have been polished smooth by centuries of flames such that it's almost impossible to tell where the gold ends and the cave begins. The unmistakable breath of the ancient beast fills the air, warming and cooling the wind in rhythm. Erphin shields his friend with an invisibility spell, making the intent of this whole plan clear.

"You better know what you're fucking doing," whispers a nervous Plyntys.

"I told you to stay home."

Erphin preps a second spell for himself and unsheathes a dagger, the dagger carried by the assassin which no doubt still has the scent of the original killer on it. Erphin creeps up to the dragon, massive and red with a snout taller than him. A loose scale near its nostril becomes the target as Erphin unleashes his blade with full force then quickly shields himself.

The dragon stirs from its slumber infuriated by the dagger still stuck in its scales. Luckily, the invisibility spells are effective enough to keep the men hidden from the dragon. It races out of the cave in search of its attacker and begins to lay waste to the entire rival village. The two watch from the cave mouth as the village burns. Plyntys shudders at the thought of all the people dying at the hand of the dragon, but Erphin grins with relief and malice.

"There," Erphin points at the village leader running for his horse. "He mustn't be allowed to survive."

Erphin and Plyntys leave the cave far behind and race for their horses. They spot the enemy leader and his men fleeing the village just as the dragon swoops in after one of the henchmen. He is grabbed by the dragon and carried back to its lair. While some around the leader are burned by the dragon, he escapes unscathed.

The rival group watches in horror as their friend is carried away and they fail to notice Plyntys and the vengeful father who have ridden up to them and dismounted to sneak up to them. Plyntys represses a surge of guilt as he nods in agreement to Erphin. Both men unleash a violent fire spell on their opponents that turns them to ash and will hopefully look like dragon fire. They make sure to burn the grass and buildings in the same way a dragon would in an attempt to hide their tracks.

Vengeance has been achieved, but a cost possibly too great to bear. Plyntys is swarmed with visions of Erphin becoming a dragon and burning entire landscapes, even boiling lakes with his flames. Plyntys shoves away his fears of this future and whether he will help make it a reality by supporting his friend. He decides to continue his silence and the two men ride home with an unspoken agreement to never mention this day again.

Plyntys hardly speaks a word on the way home and droops his head with a faraway stare while he processes what has just occurred. Erphin sits up tall with a smirk on his face as he replays the day's events back through his mind. Plyntys notices severe burns on Erphin's arm, burns he suffered when performing such an advanced fire spell without the proper training.

"Your arm, it looks painful," says Plyntys.

"Nothing the Surgeon can't fix, and nothing I wouldn't suffer ten times over to keep my family safe. Let's take the route through the forest, the village thinks we went to hunt deer after all."

The man prepares his bow for the second hunt of the day while humming a tune to himself. Plyntys has another vision of flames engulfing the forest near their village, flames that seem to feed the evil hunger of the forest rather than burn it down. A decrepit shell of Erphin stands in the middle of the flames, laughing maniacally and chanting. The vision consumes the thoughts of Plyntys the whole ride home, leaving him concerned for the wellbeing of his friend and the whole village.

Turmoil

Erphin's home village buzzes with fear and excitement in preparation for the arrival of the king as he passes through to the capital of a neighboring nation. Ten years have passed since Erphin and Plyntys silently destroyed a rival village by tricking a dragon into committing an atrocity. Erphin's daughter is alive thanks to that atrocity and lives with her new husband on the other side of the mountain. Erphin's wife fell victim to the harsh winter five years ago, leaving him lonely, brooding, and determined to fulfill the promise he made to her in her last moments. Erphin's face and hair have aged considerably, no doubt due to his obsession with practicing dangerous spells out near the forest. His eyes have darkened and his cheekbones sunken in as a result of his life force being used to heal his wounds. Plyntys disappeared two years ago after visiting the forest on his own, leaving the village to gossip about what they assume happened to him.

Shopkeepers tidy their wares over and over, food vendors toss all but the most perfect items into a bucket for the villagers to enjoy out of sight of the king. Everything must be in order. The king is unlikely to notice, but the pilot fish-like humans who make up his entourage are fickle and live for a reason to exercise even a modicum of authority over the peasants they see as less than themselves. So much work for a few hours, but the repercussions of inaction are dire.

"My father hates oranges," says a teenage prince while kicking over a fruit stand. "It's as if these peasants want to anger their king!"

The men around him laugh loudly as the prince wrecks a poor woman's entire shop.

"Please, sir!" The woman shrieks as she tries to save what's left of the fruit. "I can't afford to fix this stand, and I won't have any more fruit to sell for months. I'll hide it away where the king won't see it. Please."

The prince shoves her away and reaches for another basket to topple, but is intercepted by Erphin who blocks the way and takes a fighting stance against him. The prince steps back and smiles as he stares down the unarmed peasant fuming before him. Erphin holds his ground, but in the silence of his staredown with the prince he hears the unmistakable sounds of war around him. The stretching of bowstrings on rooftops, the clinking of armored hands unsheathing hungry broadswords, all eclipsed by the chuckle coming from the prince just waiting for a reason to tear him apart.

Protecting the village is important to Erphin, and vengeance is worth dying for, but he decides to wait for another opportunity to arise that will make his death more impactful. He turns away from the prince and begins to help the shopkeeper pick up her fruit. The prince signals to the guards to disband and he walks away with an extra level of pep to his step.

"Nothing rivals the pomposity of royalty," says Erphin to the woman.

"That may be but you'll get yourself killed if you keep that up. Thank you for helping me. The king should arrive soon, best you hide in the crowd and become forgettable."

Erphin feigns agreement and walks off to join the crowd waiting for the king's arrival. A few moments later, trumpets and criers announce the arrival of the king.

The king rides on a massive horse that allows him to easily tower over all in attendance. Though he rides through friendly territory, he is protected by thick plate armor and a magickal shield enchanted with powerful spells.

"Who is the one who would dare threaten harm to my son

and heir?" The king's voice bellows out with a fearful bassy tone. "Show yourself or I'll free the world of this useless peasant village!"

Now, this is the perfect opportunity to make a death worthwhile.

Erphin emerges from the crowd of peasants and slowly approaches the king with his head bowed. "It is I, sir. I protected a woman from the prince's poor manners."

"Poor manners?! I'll admit he's repugnant at times, but I'll not take insults from low-born filth. Come closer, so that I may remember your face."

Erphin slowly steps towards the king and makes eye contact as the king draws a long broadsword from his saddle sheath. The king lowers the magickal shield around him and begins to dismount slowly as Erphin contemplates his next move. His blood runs cold as he questions whether he can save himself by killing the king surrounded by a small army. He remembers the loss of his lover and the unending famine in his village, then decides he'd rather die today than rough out another winter as a peasant. Dreams of ancient tomes and powerful court wizards fill his head and strengthen his resolve.

Erphin leaps at the king, flipping him off his horse and smashing some of his armor on impact. The king is caught completely off guard and hardly has time to react before Erphin unsheathes a dagger. He stabs the king repeatedly in the chest, with the dagger bending more and more against the plate armor. Then he proceeds to crush the king's head against the ground over and over, removing more of his helmet.

Erphin then casts a force spell to push the guards away, just like he practiced out in the woods. A wave of panic comes over him as reality catches up to him, but he pushes it back and continues attacking the king. He creates a protective flame circle around himself and the king in the hopes of keeping others out. With his hand still flaming, he punches the king with a finishing blow. The pain is almost unbearable, but Erphin ignores it as he ends his spell and begins to realize the situation he has created. The king's bloodied body lays in front of him, as well as the crown that symbolizes power over the entire kingdom.

He grabs the crown with bloodied and burned hands and places it on his head, saying "I think this is a great fit." A smirk grows on his face, not unlike the smile he showed Plyntys during the dragon raid a decade ago. He looks at the shocked faces of the peasants and nobility alike, looking for anyone eager to join the king in his fate.

One of the king's guards, a large man in thick armor carrying a war axe, walks up to Erphin. He removes his helmet and kneels before Erphin as a sign of resignation. He nods at his fellow soldiers to signal them to do the same as dreams of gaining power flood his mind—dreams involving using this peasant's powers and ambition to his advantage.

"What are you doing?!" The prince shrieks and curses the traitor. "My father is dead and you bow before his murderer? I am your king now! This man can't be king, the kingdom won't allow it. I won't allow it!"

"I welcome the challenge, little boy," says Erphin with an increasingly smug grin. "What is a king if not the one who wears the crown? I've taken this one for myself and I have no intention of returning it to your insolent bloodline."

One of the guards loyal to the prince drags him away as the tides turn in Erphin's favor. The remaining guards and the peasants alike bow before their new king. Erphin climbs on his new horse and rides for his new throne with no interest in continuing the bureaucratic mission that caused this whole interaction.

Trespassers

"Let go of me!" A young woman shouts while trying to break free from a guard's grasp. Her dark copper skin wrinkles under the firm clutch of his strong, ash-toned hand as she squirms and kicks at his shielded legs. Her shout echoes through the grounds of the large castle, reaching the snow-capped mountains that form the valley in which the castle resides. Between her and the castle entrance stands a massive stone wall known as Keirlin's Wall. The wall is speckled with burn marks and covered in a strange residue.

The woman's warm breath condenses into a dense fog as it clashes against the freezing air around her. Her black shoulder-length locs dance across her tan tunic as she wrestles with the guard and hits him with her messenger bag.

"All trespassers must be brought before the captain of the guard," says the annoyed guard as he resists her blows with ease. He continues to pull her towards the guards' hut near the entrance to the castle.

"I'm not trespassing," she says haughtily, "I've simply *invited* myself." Just as she turns her head away from him to revel in her self-amusement, she hears metal clashing against metal. The guard's grip goes limp and she sees him fall to the ground in a puddle of his blood that soaks into the thick fur coat draped over his shoulders. She covers her mouth to hold in a surprised shriek at the sight of the murdered man in front of her.

A shadow sneaks silently into the bushes nearby—no doubt the killer, she thinks. Her blood runs cold at the thought that she could be next, but she sees the shadow quickly leap over Keirlin's Wall and execute another soldier guarding the castle entrance. The shadow enters the light and she notices it is a man in a long cloak. She wonders how a fully grown man can land so silently. He fumbles with the lock and begins to grow increasingly impatient. He does not acknowledge her, yet he is clearly aware of her as she approaches slowly and, what she considers, silently.

She closes the distance between them and is able to make out more details about the stranger. A man older than her, yet not past his prime, with broad shoulders that form the boxy shape of his brown and tattered cloak. The oddly thin cloak reveals much of his muscular form and is held together by a peculiar brooch, far too elegant for a cloak like this. The brooch is made of some kind of delicate metal and contains the most brilliant yellow gem she has ever seen. The yellow of the gem is a pleasant match to the strands of hair she can see under his hood, but not much of his face is visible.

"Fuck," he says as he drops the lock and glares at her. "You can open this, right? With the tools clinking around in your bag louder than a warhammer against a shield. Surely you wouldn't have shown up here without a plan..." He gestures at the lock with a forced smile followed by an irritated eye roll as he storms off to look for more guards to send off to the underworld.

She pauses to fire back a comment about his own lack of planning but decides to focus on getting through the door. The lock is large and hefty to hold, with a bit of rust that makes the pins that much harder to force open. She fiddles with the lock for a few moments and is eventually able to pry it open.

"See," she says with a smile, "it just needed some finesse."

"Great," he says as he reaches to open the door slowly.

"A thank you wouldn't hurt," she retorts with an offended tone.

No response, not even eye contact.

"You didn't even introduce yourself or ask my name," her volume raises as his rudeness begins to enrage her.

"That's accurate," he says in the same monotone voice before pausing, as if to see whether she will continue talking. He clicks his tongue and takes a long breath before saying, "You know they'll kill us if they find us, yeah? Your silence would be the best thing for you to contribute here."

"All trespassers must be brought before the captain of the guard," she mockingly repeats the guard's comment from earlier.

"All trespassers *found in the yard* are brought to the captain," he says while scratching his forehead. "Trespassers *found in the castle* are executed on sight. The King is to be guarded at all costs."

His last sentence sounds more like someone repeating a memorized phrase than someone issuing a warning, which stirs an odd sense of fear and curiosity in the woman. She decides to follow the man inside the castle—it's not like she can get in on her own and he hasn't killed her yet. She hopes for that trend to continue.

The entrance to the castle gives way to a massive foyer formed by thick wooden beams wrapped in intricate iron brackets. A large fire off to the left side of the room heats the equally large space and provides enough light to make out the form of two guards warming themselves with its flames. The woman turns to signal their presence to her shadowy companion, but stops as she spots him stalking the guards silently. "Hundreds of feet traveled in seconds without a single sound, how is this possible?" She thinks to herself.

The cloaked killer makes light and quiet work of both guards, hiding their bodies among the piles of firewood. They'll be discovered within the day, but he doesn't seem concerned about staying in the castle for long. Another wave of fear hits the woman as she processes not only the speed and efficiency with which this man killed two well-trained guards but also the lack of a pause to consider whether he will allow the men to live. What of their lives and families? She shakes her head and reminds herself that the alternative is her execution, but thoughts of what this man could be capable of curdle in her stomach like rotten milk.

The tenuous alliance makes its way through the foyer, through a long hallway decorated with paintings and statues of former kings, and on towards the mess hall. The hall is somehow larger than the foyer, with vaulted ceilings so high they seem to reach the heavens above and long tables surrounded by hundreds of stout chairs sturdy enough to hold the weight of heavily armored soldiers. The smooth brick walls are adorned with hunting trophies of all kinds, including magickal creatures that went extinct long ago. The woman stands in awe of the most elegant room she's ever seen, taking in the intricate carvings on each chair and wondering how beams so heavy can be supported by brackets that seem so delicate and thin. She feels a sense of pride at her first time being in the presence of such opulence.

The long table in the middle of the room is older than the castle, made by the hands of the first king of the realm from a tree he chopped down himself. The tabletop is still smooth and the legs show signs of age, but have been restored many times by the royal craftsmen.

The woman pauses a moment too long, and three guards enter the room and spot her immediately. She is unable to see her companion anywhere, and is caught trying to duck under the ancient table.

"That's what I get for trusting a stranger," she mutters to herself. "Don't come any closer!"

The guards attempt to restrain her but she retaliates by hitting the guard closest to her in the face with an extremely ornate silver plate. The plate crashes against his steel helmet, creating a loud bang that leaves him dazed just long enough for the woman to escape. Just as another guard moves to chase after the woman, all of the candles in the room flicker in an unmotivated breeze and one of the guards falls to the floor dead.

The two other guards stand back to back and look around to catch sight of the one who would dare kill a royal guard inside the castle. A second flicker of the lights and both men let out shrieks of pain followed by gurgling noises as their throats are slit. Silence fills the mess hall again and the companion appears next to his friend who is armed with her dented plate and a freshly broken table leg.

"Nice plate," he chuckles. "I suppose that works as a shield. Did you break a table in the King's castle?" He nervously checks to make sure she hasn't damaged the Table of Kings.

"Well *you* disappeared so *I* had to improvise," says the woman as she cracks a smile. "The plate was surprisingly effective, you should try it sometime."

The woman notices that her companion's cloak is more tattered than when they entered the castle, but he doesn't appear to have sustained any serious injuries. One large hole in his cloak reveals a marking on his arm, a marking not unlike the sigil plastered all over the castle and the guards' armor.

"That tattoo! Are you one of them?" She asks between labored breaths, not expecting the truth but unable to keep herself from asking. It then dawns on the woman that they are headed for the very king that bestowed the tattoo on this killer. She wants to leave but freezes as curiosity and adrenaline overtake her caution.

As the man stops and looks down at the ground to focus on the sounds around him, he clutches the peculiar brooch on his cloak. A crash erupts from an unknown source in the room next door which causes the man to crush his brooch, and the precious gem with it. An explosion of light and flame is followed by a massive gust of wind, yet nothing burns or is blown over. Another crash is heard, this one so close and so loud that the woman's ears ring, followed by the crumbling of the stones comprising a nearby wall.

When the woman's eyes have adjusted to the rapid influx of light, she sees that her companion is wearing an intricate suit of armor far more elegant and detailed than any of the awe-inspiring adornments she's seen today. His face is square and his eyes stern and angular, with short hair the same color as the crushed gem on the ground before him. He holds a long sword in his right hand and a large heater shield in his left hand, large enough to protect his even more massive body. His eyes are fixed on the newcomer, a man who tore through two feet of dense stone the way one tears paper.

The newcomer is covered by armor equally as ornate, yet his smaller frame seems less impressive than his opponent. His dark hair covers a face that is long and skinny, a shape repeated by his tall and slender figure. He holds two short blades that are without a doubt strong enough to cut through even the thick armor worn by the companion. The two soldiers square off, then unleash a flurry of steel and sparks with such speed that the woman is unable to discern any individual movements from either man. Their power is an equal match, with each man sending the other flying across the room and shattering tables, chairs, and any other furniture in their path. The only furniture strong enough to withstand the mayhem is the ancient table in the middle of the room, thanks to the many enchantments placed on it over the years.

ANIME FIGHT!

The newcomer pauses his assault after catching sight of the woman across the room.

"Interesting," he says with a smirk. "The shopkeeper's daughter, no doubt here for the King. Does she know you killed her father?"

A fresh flurry of deadly blows is the only response given.

"Careful now," says the newcomer. "I'm getting aggravated. She probably thinks I meant it was an accident. Ate his liver, didn't you? A humble shopkeeper going about his day, struck down by a high knight of the royal guard. Stripped for parts, boiled for the mad wizard's potions. Keirlin's potion has increased your strength, I see. Was the shopkeeper *really* so ordinary, I wonder?"

"Hey!" The woman shouts as she throws her recently weaponized tableware at the highly trained warrior. The assailant swats the plate away, distracting him from the companion for a split second.

"Is that a plate—"

The assailant is caught unaware by the companion's deft slice to his throat and left to bleed out on the floor. The champion walks off quickly, paying no heed to the woman who helped him win the fight, not that he had before.

"Oh come on," she says. "The plate saved the day again."

No response from her companion.

"I hated my father," she attempts to get his attention again.

"I don't care," says the companion as he walks to the King's door. "The lock needs picking."

"And what if I don't pick it?"

"You will. It's why you're here today, Aynorra. To confront the King, your distant relative and the one responsible for ordering your father's death. You may even be curious whether you're next on his list."

She is hit with a sense of numbness, shock, and rage all at the same time. "How do you know about my family?!!"

"Do you *really* think I'd show up without a plan?!" His first genuine smile of the day. "Your father's blood was clearly royal, the taste is too unique to miss. Come come now, pick the lock. Most people do as they're told."

His eyes dart around looking for more guards to fight, more throats to slit. His agitation grows with each second and Aynorra can feel her throat climbing to the top of his list. She realizes that if they are discovered he could easily flee, leaving her to a fate of certain death. She decides to pick the lock, which is a far more easy task than she expected for a lock protecting the King. Aynorra's sense of confusion grows as they creep into the King's chamber.

The King is asleep, as usual, behind a magickal shield powered by the mad court wizard. Aynorra's companion approaches the shield, drawing his sword from its sheath. He stands tall with his sword in front of him and mutters some words to himself under his breath, causing his armor and sword to glow the same color as the magick protecting the King. He turns towards the magickal shield and slowly slides his sword into it, stabbing the sleeping King through the chest. The King awakens with a cry as the companion twists the sword deeper into his heart. He pulls his sword out, flooding the bed and floor with the precious blood of the King as the magickal shield disintegrates. The King's death is known immediately to the wizards of the kingdom, and the sound of horns rings out from all around the castle.

He sheaths his sword and pulls out a large crate next to the King's bed. A look of panic comes over the man's face, something not seen during any of the battles from today or even when slaughtering the sleeping King. He opens the crate tenderly and pulls out a large terrified dog with long wiry black hair. The dog sniffs the man and immediately begins to lick him as he recognizes his friend.

"I know buddy, it's ok now," he says to the shaking dog while nuzzling his face into the dog's fur. "I told the King not to take you from me. I did! I warned him!"

The man pauses to look over at Aynorra and pats her awkwardly on the shoulder then looks at the bloody corpse of the King. He grabs the crown with his free hand, wipes off some of the blood on his armor, and hands it to her.

"Well, that's that. Enjoy the crown. May your neck be strong enough to bear the weight and stay forever attached to your shoulders. Cheer up, you get to meet the captain of the guard, just like you wanted." He says while walking towards a nearby window to make his escape.

"Are you kidding me?!" Aynorra screams as she's left in complete shock and afraid for her life. "You killed him and you're just going to leave me here?! What do you mean about the crown?"

"Oh, you don't listen," he says with a second smirk. "Most people do as they're told. You can just pick up the crown and wear it if you want to. Your father had royal blood, after all. Farewell!"

He walks off to the window, pulls a cleverly disguised lever, and escapes through a hidden passage meant for the King to use during an emergency. The tunnel closes behind him, leaving Aynorra with nothing but the crown and a crippling sense of fear and uncertainty. One thing she is certain of is that she will never see that man again—she has a feeling that he left none alive capable of tracking him down.

As guards fill the royal chamber, Aynorra pauses in fear but then remembers that she must keep her composure if she wishes to keep her head. She places the crown on her head and raises a hand to the soldiers to signal them to stop their charge.

"The murderer, my kidnapper, has fled. Go find him!" She orders with confidence that shocks her.

The guards pause in confusion and look to their captain for guidance. The captain takes a moment to process the scene in front of him—the dead King in his bed with no magickal shield, the picked lock laying on the ground next to him, and the lone woman standing confidently before him. Being a strong believer in fate and the Will of the gods, the captain decides to leave her fate to the higher powers.

"We'll leave her to the wizards," says the captain. "She did open the unpickable lock, after all. She must have royal blood. Send the guards into the forest to look for the murderer."

Aynorra winces for a second after realizing that she didn't pick the last lock. It opened for her, for the blood in her veins—the blood that got her father killed and the blood her companion needed to complete his plan. Rather than focus on feeling used, she smiles at the thought that she now stands before the very captain she spent hours avoiding and is about to give him orders.

"Find him and bring him to me, you'll do as you're told. You may find me on my throne," says the Queen as she walks towards the throne room.

Green Hood

A violent thunderstorm crashes down on a large, thirty room country house, causing the tall spires on the rooftops to cast frantic shadows across the estate. The gardens are void of the usual servants, but none can miss the plethora of armed guards who took their place. Shining steel plates cover the men from head to toe, turning them into one incoherent mass of lightning fodder, but they're needed tonight—there's a meeting happening in the library and the guest list is strict. Swords and maces catch glimpses of moonlight as some of the guards swing them around to burn off their boredom, experience breeds focus. The inside of the house is dark everywhere but the library, where the candlelight pours out of the windows to flood the lawn with warmth.

In the corner of the west garden, among the tall cypress bushes, a hooded figure cloaked in dark green from head to toe waits in the shadows unaffected by the rain and her own impatience. No time to fuck around, she's here to carry out the mission given to her by the head of her clan, and the oldest assassin in town. She was told about the sale happening in the library and figures she can snag the relic for herself as a bonus reward after completing the actual mission. She's been tasked with stabbing the seller, the new heir to the Grantson family, with a knife stolen from the buyer's hometown of Makart to blame it on the buyer. Starting a war between powerful families always fetches a high price tag. Killing the young Mr Grantson isn't required so long as the buyer is blamed and a war ensues, but it is often the outcome as anonymity is paramount. Captured assassins don't grow old.

She uses the lightning strikes as her cue to move through the gardens towards the house. Through the wildflower garden and around the fish pond she goes to jump onto a pergola over the rose bushes. Then, she leaps from the roof during the next strike, landing silently in the rose bushes below. Crack, she leaps from behind a bush with a dart coated in a sleeping potion to strike a man standing guard, managing to flee before the light dissipates. Twice more she takes out the guards before they can see her and sneaks into the building through an open awning window near the kitchen.

Her shadow dances in the flickering light of the hallway candles while she stalks her way to the library. Another lightning strike reveals her position to a silhouetted man outside the window. With no time for sleeping potions, she draws her bow and hardly has time to line up the shot before firing an arrow through the window and into the face of the guard. Right between the eyes.

Fuck, that was close. She thinks to herself.

He falls backwards into the bushes, leaving only bits of her arrow and its fletching visible. Fletching from the town of Makart, just like the stolen dagger. The devil is in the details.

On to the main event, the assassination and framing. She

enters the library unnoticed and takes note of the occupants. Two of the buyer's guards on the far side, by the large leather chairs and the sheepskin bound philosophy books—from Grantson's time in the southern islands. Both have long swords held out in front of them, with the tip resting on their steel boots as a show of respect for the old wood flooring. Neither is much larger than the assassin, but their thick armor trades speed and flexibility for complete coverage and durability. Their only vulnerabilities are their faces and a small spot on the wrist where one could disarm the men.

Three more brutes from the seller's side stand on the wall nearest the door, big hulking masses with sparse leather armor. Armor like this would seem careless in comparison if it weren't for their brutish weapons, a clear death sentence for anyone who crosses them. The two on the outside hold large black iron maces in one hand with the other hand resting on the hilt of sheathed scimitars. No shields for these men, they're hired to kill and shields would slow them down. The middle guard, taller than the others and possibly the largest man the assassin has ever seen, stands empty-handed with a massive warhammer on the ground in front of him. The large, ornate head of the hammer and the telltale spike on the other side mean this could only be one man. One who folks call the Bear Killer.

Shit. How unexpected.

Legend says he's thrown a fully grown bear with one hand and that even swords bend across his bare chest. Exaggerations spread by soldiers or war magick brewed and bottled as potions to make warriors invincible? Now isn't the time to indulge curiosity, no matter how fascinating the subject. In battle, he uses the hammer head to build up enough momentum to drive the spike through an opponent's shield, through their armor and into whichever organs are foolish enough to be in his way. The unstoppable man's tree trunks of arms are folded in front of him, his head tilted down slightly to reinforce the scowl on his face. He won't be easy to dispatch or distract. A mercenary with that price tag is a quiet show of wealth from the seller, yet also an unconscious intimidation tactic used for bartering.

The man they came to protect, the seller and owner of the Grantson estate himself, is seated just in front of his guards in the nicest armchair in the room. The man is not much older than the assassin, younger than one would expect to own such a house, but early inheritance is common for a black market dealer. Power always claims its price. For all the griefs that weigh on this man, not a trace of victimhood is noticeable in his strong jaw or piercing eyes, nor is it easy to miss the strength emanating from his perfectly proportional shoulders. His hands are stronger than one would expect from a man who has known wealth his entire life. He looks as if he could wield a sword and parry a full strike.

Maybe he gets to live, just maybe.

A foil to the appeal and calm confidence of the seller sits across from him, a fool adorned in all manner of jewelry, a ruffled linen shirt, and ill-fitted silk breeches with a floral pattern. This loud and shiny lavishness is a clear sign of new money, contrasted by the quiet show of old wealth whispered by the massive library full of exotic books and priceless artifacts.

The fool bumbles through his haggling to talk down the price, though his sweaty brow and repeated phrases show that this deal is about to close in favor of his adversary.

The negotiations won't last much longer, time for a plan.

The buyer half-heartedly mumbles a story about the King himself telling him that the relic is already his property and thus there's no need for a sale.

"Do you have this in writing?" Asks Grantson.

"No, it was told to my men by a messenger." The words almost fail to pour out of the fool's shivering mouth.

"The King's messenger Alphara?" A question that answers itself as his messages are always accompanied by royal parchment.

"No, one of his captains sent a messenger boy only a few days ago," squeals the buyer as he throws his hands out to the side, seemingly shrugging off his answer as he gave it.

"Riiiiight." A smirk surreptitiously erupts on the face of the Bear Killer as the seller gets a dig in on the buyer. Grantson's hands tremble with aggravation and eagerness to shut this man up, but he bides his time.

"My price will only increase with further haggling," says the seller with a stern look and a slight head tilt. "What do you say?"

The plan, the plan. Ah, an archer from the seller's side in the balcony above. An easy target for a skilled archer. Perfect. Escape? Shit. The only awning windows in here are in the clerestory over 30 feet up. It'll be the door near the kitchen again, then. Now to forge a motive for the killing of Grantson's man.

The assassin coats a pebble in a bewilderment potion and flicks it at the shin of the buyer, not that he needs another reason to be obscene and inflammatory but he isn't making enough of a scene. She knocks a devilishly detailed stolen arrow and draws it silently, waiting for a cue.

"YOU WOULD DARE DEFY THE KING?!!" Shouts the buyer with strength and confidence that shocks even his men.

The buyer becomes enraged and orders his men to take out one of the guards as punishment for this treason, but a guard in the balcony, seemingly their captain, quickly orders against it. A second smirk from Bear Killer, but this one is more lustful than amused. The assassin looses her arrow on the next lightning crash and the archer on the balcony falls over dead. His neighbor sounds the alarm and begins to fire at the archers across the room on the assumption that they fired on them. The ringing of steel erupts as weapons are unsheathed and the unmistakable sound of bows being drawn signals the beginning of the bloodbath.

Absolute fucking chaos, hell yeah.

Green Hood knows that Bear Killer has no reason to leave his post, as the two men across the room can be handled by his wingmen and even the archers in the balcony seem to be scared to confront him. This won't do. She looses another arrow right into the neck of the guard closest to her without the cover of a lightning strike. The seller and Bear Killer develop a quick blank stare, with their eyes ever slightly turned in her direction—

giving the sense that they turned their attention towards her without looking at her, the same way a hunter tracks a deer without letting the deer know it's been noticed.

Their attention is stolen as one of the buyer's guards shouts and swings his sword at the seller. Bear Killer catches the blade with his hand, ignoring the blood rushing down his forearm, and pulls the guard in for a headbutt. Skull against steel, but this time the skull wins. The guard stumbles back and tries to regain his balance as Bear Killer lands a chest-crushing kick that collapses his armor and sends the man flying back into the books behind him, easily fifteen feet. A single ringing noise signals that the warhammer has left the ground and is being swung in the direction of the second guard.

"Mind the poetry, B.K." Grantson orders as he pats the behemoth on the shoulder condescendingly. "Those volumes are hard to come by." No response from the man swinging a hundred pounds of steel with murderous intent.

Another blank stare forms on the seller's face as he looks out the window just over the assassin's shoulder. He draws a deep breath and releases it with a sigh and a nod as if convincing himself to proceed with whatever his brain is telling him to do. He turns around and stares at the sniveling buyer crawling on the floor to avoid the battle. No action, he just stares and waits for something but gives no hints as to what that could be.

Fuck it.

The green-hooded assassin draws her stolen dagger and creeps up behind the man with a blank stare. She spots a gap in his armor where the servants missed a buckle, that'll do. The war is almost inevitable at this point and killing a battle-trained noble with a piercing gaze and a poetry collection seems unnecessary. Maybe he will require a trained assassin to take revenge on his assailant, it's not impossible. Another crack of lightning and the steel slides into the armor gap then pulls out a fair amount of blood on its exit. The assassin lands her leap behind a broken chair and watches as Grantson the nobleman falls to his knees clutching his side with an almost belabored cry, then catches sight of the buyer next to him.

"You stabbed me!" Grantson cries loud enough to ensure the whole room hears him.

"I, I would never!" Retorts the buyer between his gasps and manic shivering.

The nobleman draws his sword and plunges it into the heart of the buyer without any hesitation. No amount of dim lighting could cover the smile growing on his face as he watches the buyer bleed out and go limp. The assassin grabs the ancient relic from within the wreckage of the room, then sneaks out the door and through the window she entered. The fighting has brought the exterior guards towards the front door of the house, leaving none to stop her exit. In a flash, she is off the property and walking briskly back to her hideout.

Almost too easy.

The following morning, the assassin paces her hideout waiting for word from her clan leader on how to collect her reward. The waiting is easy, but her mind is racing thinking about the man she stabbed the night before. He must have seen her, he looked right at her with his piercing eyes as he clenched his sharp jaw. Why didn't he say something? No, he must have been too distracted by all the fighting to see her hidden in the shadows. No one just ignores someone hiding in a room when a fight breaks out. Maybe she looked like a blanket or a pile of books. But she can't ignore the feeling she had when he looked towards her, the rush of her heart and the fear of being caught. Her pulse quickens even now as she recalls the event. Best not to dwell on it.

Early afternoon, finally. She leaves her apartment to collect her dead drop, which is usually full of payment and sometimes offers for more work, but this one has a note. A note! It apologizes for the break in procedure, then instructs her to meet on the roof of the big church at sunset.

Why? This isn't how these things work. Maybe someone wants the ugly statue back, it doesn't even seem to be enchanted. Probably won't fetch much on the streets anyway.

Sunset approaches as the assassin reaches the church rooftop to meet her boss and collect payment. No boss to be seen.

Bad feelings.

She turns to leave quickly and bumps into what feels like a wall where there definitely wasn't one before. She looks up to see the face of none other than fucking Bear Killer himself smiling at her while bouncing his death hammer in his hands. His head gestures back behind her where Grantson is holding a bag. Just large enough to fit her head and just where she doesn't want her head to end up. She stands motionless in shock, going limp as the big asshole behind her nudges her forward like a pirate walking a sailor off the plank. She takes a breath and stands upright to make a case for herself, but the nobleman holds out his hand and interjects.

"You put on quite the show," he says with a glare and a raised eyebrow that blends into the hairs that fall on his forehead.

"I always do."

"I assume you'll want payment beyond what you stole for yourself. It's a fake, by the way. The real one glows in the moonlight. I thought you were trained in magick." The last sentence ends with a chuckle as he tosses the bag at her feet.

The thud of the bag and jingle of coins, that's a nice sound.

"Did you pay me to stab you?" She jeers. "I can inflict all sorts of pain for the right size coin purse."

A slight raise of the eyebrows and a twitch of the head from the nobleman as he stands up from his perch on the parapet. His reaction disappears as he focuses on his purpose.

"My donations to the King's guard have somewhat lessened my fortunes, and I've never liked that prick. War is profitable, as I'm sure you know, and that fool from last night has money that I'm in need of. I could use your work soon, though I'll ask that you keep my bleeding to a minimum."

"That's a shame, skin like yours is the most fun to toy with."

"Keep your toying to my adversaries and B.K. will let you keep your head attached. Go now and wait for word from your boss on what I want next. Oh, and use the front door next time. Those mercenaries are fucking expensive."

Green Hood

Bear Killer steps aside to let the assassin sneak off into the shadows and return home, the long way to avoid any unwanted followers. As she sneaks off into the streets, she can't help but wonder what could happen the next time she sees the nobleman. He is confusing, yet oddly alluring and unlike the other nasty nobles she's dealt with in the past.

Best to keep a good distance from him on future jobs, trust issues are a job requirement after all.

A Meaningful Obsession

It is only after time is given to a failed quest for the meaning of things that we can discover the inherent meaninglessness of these same things. Yet, the burning desire to complete this quest breeds an obsession, an obsession which in turn gives meaning to the time spent exploring the meaninglessness. A meaningful obsession with meaningless things. Such is the meaning of life.

Grab the Booty

Just after dawn, tall grasses breathe fog into the morning air as an army marches along a path carved through the plains. The marching boots echo through the valley, with the noise reaching the putrid swamps to the south. The column of soldiers surround armored cargo carts carrying mostly gold and gems, but with a few rare items of arcane origins—hence the dozen or so powerful sorcerers riding on the wagons. The army is composed of large and fearsome mercenaries known as Palkrins. Palkrins are mostly human, but are reminiscent of both rhinos and crocodiles, with thick skin of varying shades of gray and taupe and large protruding teeth lining their snouts.

A soldier on the edge of the column carelessly swings his sword through the grass to alleviate his boredom. As he swipes through a tuft of grass, his blade connects with the face of a hidden bandit. The bandit shouts in pain while another leaps from the grass to impale the soldier with his dagger.

One, two, three strikes with the dagger, with the third swipe cutting through the soldier's coif and into his thick neck. Horns and trumpets of all sorts sound through the field to make the skirmish known. Hundreds of elite stalkers emerge from the grass to ambush the convoy!

A shield dome is formed around the covered wagons by the

assemblage of sorcerers hired to guard the booty, a barrier strong enough to block almost all known practitioners of the magickal arts. The soldiers outside the barrier form a wall with their metal shields, not lacking even in the shadow of a nearly impenetrable wall of pure magick.

Palkrin warriors carry a steel shield three inches thick that covers them from head to toe and has spikes used for offensive attacks or anchoring the shield into the ground. Their armor is made of hundreds of small scales and outward-facing spikes. The sheer amount of dense metal brings the weight of the equipment, and the beast below it, to something near an elephant's weight—Palkrins average about seven feet tall which is why they are often hired for these guardian missions.

The Palkrin battalion moves as one, thrusting their shields out in unison to push their enemies back as they step forward over piles of fallen bodies. Meanwhile, Palkrins armed with halberds and poleswords reach out from behind the shield wall to hack at those closest to them. The enemy stalkers are armed with long-reaching spears and high-powered bows with arrows meant to penetrate soft spots in armor. Their onslaught weakens the shield wall considerably and almost breaks through two spots in the line before being pushed back by reinforcements. The fresh Palkrins manage to surround most of the stalker army and either crush or stab them to death.

Just as it seems the stalkers will lose horribly, their cavalry rides in on armored Dvoarks, magickal creatures akin to a spotted bear-boar hybrid with a cat-like tail, to dismantle the shield wall. The Palkrins are powerful, yet weak in comparison to these massive beasts. Even with the Palkrins gone, the rogue army seems to have nothing powerful enough to bring down the magick shield and secure their prize of riches.

The carts inside the magickal shield begin to tremble and shake as the giant swamp drakes of the south, acid-breathing lizards over eighty feet long, appear on both ends of the convoy. Three per squad, the nasty lizards unleash a breath attack that fluctuates between a boiling liquid, sparks, and a true flame, yet is also seemingly all three things at once. The flames stick to the shield and begin to eat through the wall while the stalkers and their cavalry prepare to battle more Palkrin reinforcements.

A cavalry captain from the stalker army climbs on a pile of armor and bodies to address the fighters. She is short with tawny skin and long, dark hair pulled back into a tight bun. She commands her warriors to dig a defensive trench and surround it with a wall to protect against the reinforcements. They begin to collect Palkrin shields and cut down trees to build the fortifications. The Dvoark riders grab spears and swords from the dead to attach to the back of their saddles with the points dug into the ground. Then, they move in a ring shape to dig the outer edge of the trenches. The fresh dirt is quickly shoveled by the infantrymen and tossed onto the new shield wall, with the tallest and most secure section of the wall covering the actions of the death breather drakes. The improvised wall is almost a half mile long and is tall enough to protect the stalkers from spears and arrows.

After hours of digging and laying siege to the wall, fire breath wins over magick as the barrier gives way to herds of stalker warriors ambushing the sorcerers and seizing control of the carts. The elite cavalry troops riding on the drakes dismount to attach the carts to their saddles. Once this is done, they climb back on the massive lizards and begin to race away at full speed, followed closely by a squad of Dvoarks devoted to their protection.

As they exit, the fresh reinforcements of Palkrins begin to surround their enemy and clash with the forces still outside the barrier. The stalkers manage to push the reinforcements back to make room for the heisted booty to escape, never to be seen again by the Palkrins or the wealthy owners of the cargo. The rest of the stalker army retreats once the booty is secured.

Their job is done!

Vampyr Killer

A shadowy figure sits in the corner of a hostel room opposite the door while chanting quietly in a foreign tongue that sounds vaguely Latin. He drinks from an old bottle wrapped in dirty twine, rope used to attach it to his belt, and is clearly becoming sicker from its contents. He coughs after drinking and appears to be getting weaker. The figure is cloaked in a thick hooded robe made of leather that covers his face and contrasts against the sacred amulet that hangs from his golden necklace. The amulet bears symbols from an older religion practiced by priests in a remote village far from here.

He shares the hostel with a group of travelers, travelers who are more than wary of this seemingly drunken stranger. They shoot fearful glances his way to see what he will do, but the stranger is completely immobile save for drinking from the bottle.

"What do we do? I don't trust him," says one of the travelers, a young woman with curly auburn hair and olive skin.

"He's just getting drunk," says another traveler, a taller man with dark brown hair and the same olive skin, with a shrug. "It's not like he does anything. He can hear you talking about him but isn't doing anything about it. Let's just get some sleep and we can leave in the morning."

"I don't know how I'm supposed to sleep with *that man* sitting there..." The woman's muttered words trail off as she rolls over to face away from him.

The onlookers disband and lay in their beds in an attempt to sleep. After what seems like hours of chanting, all the candles in the room go out instantaneously. Then, an unmotivated flame lights the candle closest to the stranger and dances from candle to candle throughout the room as if hunting something on the other side of the wall. The drunken stranger stops chanting, watches the flame intently and moves his hand around the bottle while murmuring something new. He slowly rises from his seat and takes a wide stance, as if bracing for an impact. The few others in the room who are still awake watch with equal parts awe and fear to see what this fool will do next.

Suddenly, a form bursts through the wall and is stopped by a shield of light surrounding the chanter. The form is that of a creature taller than a human, with pale skin and large fangs covered in blood. The creature pushes harder and the chanter shouts louder. The shield dissipates, allowing the creature to push forward, and the chanting stranger breaks his bottle on the creature's face which causes it to shriek in pain as its skin boils and burns.

The chanter pulls out a small dagger and uses it to cut into the heart of the beast, dropping it to the floor in a puddle of boiling blood. As the chanter grabs the head of the assailant and cuts it off, the beast ignites and burns away, leaving few remains.

The group is fully awake now and they begin to shout and freak out—they can't get blood off their belongings. The beast killer grabs a new bottle of water and pours it onto the stains, causing them to boil away without trace. He starts to drink more as the tall traveler steps forward to ask the questions they are all thinking.

"What the hell was that? That can't be real!"

"Do you claim to know all things?"

"What? No..."

"Yet all things exist all the same, without your knowledge or permission. That was a visit from a new thing."

The chanter snaps his fingers and the flame jumps from the candle to his fingertips. He lights a piece of paper and places the flame in a jar attached to his belt. Then, he lights a new torch with a knife and flint, which he uses to relight a candle held by one of the group members.

"Didn't seem new to you," says the man. "Your words, they seemed familiar and spoke of the gods, yes?"

"In a sense. I speak of the origins of the stories that people tell each other to teach humanity how to be. I speak of things that have become known as gods and devils. The forces that control our beings and change our surroundings. I speak of pure Will."

"Will? Like a desire to fuck or eat cake?"

"No, you stupid bastard. The unconscious gravity that pulls at each of us and guides our journey through the sea of life. The Will. A force that can guide even evolution over thousands of years. The bird willed to fly, and one day it did. As the bird granted itself wings these beasts granted themselves life, eternity at any cost. They evolved from humans at some point yet are unable to exist without us, thus we are an extant species. Free range and unaware."

"How did you do that? Kill it so easily."

"I willed it."

"Teach me. I could be a hero like you."

"I am but a student."

"Who are you? You're no mere human."

"I'm no more alive than they, my heart beats no more than theirs, yet I am called a hero because I fight for humans. The contents of this bottle keep my Will intact and allow me to control my body. It is not for those who are untrained, it would be but poison to you."

The stranger runs out of the hostel through the front door and disappears into the fog. One of the group members chases after him, but quickly loses sight of their savior. The group is left in their hostel with an unbelievable story to tell and no proof to show for it.

Atansha

Coronation

In an old castle bordering on ruin, battered with age, covered in withered plants and vines hardly clinging to life, a crowd gathers in a courtyard facing a stairwell. The atmosphere is anxious and riddled with grief over the recent loss of the king —a rough leader whose ancestors let the capital building fall into ruin and removed all magickal plants and animals from within their borders. The crowd isn't here to mourn, however, for today is the coronation of the future queen Atansha, the usurper responsible for ending the reign of her predecessor. The emotions of the crowd range from anger, or joy, at the murder of their ruler, to fear and confusion about their futures. For all the king's issues, he was familiar, and that's enough for those who fear change above all else.

Shouts erupt from the crowd as they're forced to wait.

"This usurper must face a trial in front of the gods!" A middle-aged man with skin as light as his hair cries out louder than the others while sloshing his tankard of ale. "She must not be allowed to kill our king and get away with it!"

"Atansha *is* a god!" Retorts a younger noble wearing freshly cut clothes bearing her new house sigil and colors. "What right do we have to deny her Will?"

"Yeah, fuck off Martin, ya dirty old bastard! You only care about the deals you made with the king to sell your wares in the palace." The shout comes from a low-born male holding up his hand to cover his mouth, a man who has no business insulting those of the higher class but can't help but get caught up in the commotion. He quickly retreats to another place in the crowd out of fear of being discovered. Though the nobles argue over the "rightful ruler," they can always agree on punishing impertinence among the commoners.

The discourse won't escalate to violence, not in the presence of the well-armed guards spread throughout the courtyard. Even without the ruler present any form of violence within the castle is treated as a rebellion against the crown. Not even the most unruly among those loyal to the dead king would dare face Atansha directly—the stories of her feats in the recent battles have already spread throughout the region. These stories of her rebellion have instilled an equal sense of fear and curiosity in the townsfolk.

The crowd quickly quiets as a figure runs down the steps into the courtyard. Alas, it is not the queen, only the royal crier announcing her arrival. Her proclamation leaves the entire crowd silent as they wait for the first glimpse of their new queen, the woman possessing an ethereal beauty paired with a physical strength beyond even the strongest of soldiers. A woman who overthrew the king and crushed castle walls without assistance.

The abrupt silence gives way to a slow and steady tapping of shoes descending the stairs. The foliage and flowers near the stairwell bloom with life and glow with the signature verdigris hue of Atansha's magick. She is in no rush to reach the bottom of the stairs, a fact made clear by how long the crowd is given nothing but the sound of her heels and a euphonious song slowly increasing in volume. Centuries of waiting for this moment have bred no sense of haste in her.

Those in the front of the crowd gasp as they gain sight of her shoes and eventually her calves and dress. She has soft dark-golden skin that glows in the evening light and keeps its hue even among the strong magickal light emanating from her many tattoos—tattoos from which living plants grow. The dress is a vibrant and deep shade of green, yet the movement of the pattern on it leaves those who see it to wonder if the dress exists at all or whether it is formed by the plants themselves. Plants growing from the dress form a long train flowing behind her.

The thin dress obscures much of her flesh, yet shows off the form of her strong thighs that lead to her wide hips and accent the gentle curve that traces up her whole body. Gaps in the pattern hint at her skin beneath and the magickal markings covering her body. As she descends the stairs, a cloak made entirely of leaves, ferns, and flowers can be seen dancing behind her, its boxy and harsh shape further accenting her sweeping curves and ethereal presence. The slow sway of her hips leads up to an ample bust that peeks out above the top of the dress between bare shoulders, save for the mounting points of the cloak.

Her sharp collarbone and strong shoulders connect to her

arms and hands, one of which caresses the stone rail of the staircase and the other fiddles with a large gold coin bearing a strange symbol on it. The coin passes in front of her chest, catching the attention of any eyes that have never left the warm softness of her breast, as it is lifted to her face for closer inspection. Her large green eyes are fixed on the coin and pay no attention to the crowd gathered to watch her coronation. Above her eyes sits an elegant, yet modest, diadem adorned with carvings that resemble branches of a tree. The crown protrudes from a wavy thicket of hair consisting mostly of browns, deep reds, and purples, but not without an occasional pink or green that stands out in the same way a flower attracts pollinators.

It's abnormal for one to already be wearing a crown at a coronation, but that doesn't matter to Atansha. Today is a formality, in her mind she became queen long ago. Below her eyes sits a small button nose nestled between two pronounced cheekbones which lead to ears adorned with multiple piercings, each filled with dazzling jewelry and rare gemstones. Her wide and heart-shaped lips are the color of a vibrant red flower and move with a certain grace as they voice the words to her song. The rustle of her hair and cloak provide a nice juxtaposition to the soft sway rippling through her body with each careful step.

Atansha reaches the foot of the steps and gazes around at the faces awaiting her arrival. She pauses briefly to give time for some customary action to take place but grows bored of the silence and lets out a wide-eyed look while she sighs and turns to walk away.

"Any words for your queen while you have my attention?" She says with a quick turn of her head to look across the crowd.

None respond, save for the crier who approaches Atansha to relieve her of the duty of hosting. "The ceremony has concluded, my queen. You need not toil here any longer," she says.

"Good," says Atansha, "I have work to do." As she leaves the courtyard, her hands sweep across the wall of the castle as if to assure the building that it is ok now. Plants spring from the spots she touches, bearing the most beautiful flowers and sweet berries. These berries will soon be used to create a wine used as a powerful healing potion.

Rebellion

In the days leading up to her coronation, at a time when none in the kingdom know of Atansha or her strength, Atansha approaches a castle unannounced. The sound of horns fill the morning air as the single unwelcome guest approaches. A sight like this isn't usually cause for such alarm, but there is nothing usual about this intruder. This intruder is a woman who walks onto a battlefield without weapons or armor, wearing her signature green dress adorned with foliage and flowers that seem to grow out of her very being. A woman who wears her own crown to a battle against the standing king. A woman who trades battle cries for a lovely serenade that causes her various tattoos to glow a brilliant shade of bluish-green and bring the natural world around her to life. The act isn't brash or even brave, as bravery requires a feeling of fear to overcome, but rather a matter-of-fact show of strength and power. Many of the soldiers refuse to fight as they battle with the conflicting feelings of being in awe of her ethereal beauty and charisma while also terrified of what her unfathomable powers could be capable of.

As a flurry of arrows fly at her and crash into a wall of earth raised by her song, the archers are grasped by ominous vines that restrain their movement and are impervious to flame. As the arrows fail, some of the swordsmen rush in to challenge the solo warrior but are met with her greatest show of strength. She carelessly throws men across the battlefield and conjures stone armor to deflect the steel. The armor only lasts as long as the strikes from the weapons and is stronger than the steel of the blades. She is completely unmoved by the force of their strikes, the way a stone wall is unmoved by a shove from a human. The only soldiers left alive are those who surrender to her Will and stand down or begin to fight for her, to capture the king. Loyalty gained through a show of force isn't to be trusted for long, but their loyalty is only needed long enough to win the battle and gain the kingdom.

The battle ends and Atansha makes her way to the castle, but is stopped by the portcullis which was lowered to prevent her from reaching the king who recently retreated behind the large walls.

"I'm happy to let myself in, though if you would open it for me it would reduce damage to my castle and prevent further frustration on my part." Atansha speaks in a booming voice that signals the first break in her song and shakes the earth around her.

The portcullis begins to open but is quickly dropped back down as the ropes are cut by the few soldiers still loyal to the king. The gate of old is massive, large enough to let in the largest beasts of the old days—days before the king's ancestors hunted them to extinction and banished those who fought for their survival. However, the incomprehensible weight of hundreds of feet of steel doesn't slow Atansha as she flings it over her head with a single hand while the other hand keeps her hair safe from getting caught in the rough and dirty steel. The steel crashes into the earth behind her with a force that cracks some of the nearby stones and bends the teeth of the gate.

"Shame," says Atansha as she caresses the broken stone, birthing luscious plants at the site where her hand meets the rock in an attempt to heal the cracks.

"Where is your king, soldier?" The invading beauty questions a cowering mass of steel and flesh.

The soldier points to the palace on top of the hill, which is surrounded by a small group of the king's bodyguards who were without doubt promised gold and lands for their loyalty. Atansha makes her way to the palace slowly, as if on a morning stroll, taking in the familiar sights of the vendor booths and the myriad of houses filled with commoners born to the same class as her. Her song breathes life into the dead planters and unkempt gardens in an attempt to restore them to the beauty she remembers from her youth, centuries ago. Memories of playing with friends in the gardens, among plants and animals forgotten by the present kingdom for over two hundred years, fill her mind as she casually walks towards the king. The grief over the loss of her youth brings about a sadness that overwhelms her so much that a few tears roll down her soft cheek and drop onto the ground, leaving behind a small sapling that will one day turn into a powerful and old tree.

The grief soon turns into rage and determination, as it had done long ago when Atansha started her quest for vengeance and vowed to attain the powers of a deity, and her song once again stops. Her pace quickens as she races towards the palace and leaps over the guards stationed out front, bursting through the walls of the building. The guards are left stunned at her strength as she tears through more interior walls and into the room where the king is hiding. His guards are subdued by her powerful vines. As the king is bound and brought before her, a torrent of emotions crosses her face. Anger, excitement, confusion, fear, relief, grief, and so many more. Each pull at her delicate features as they clamor for control. Atansha calms her mood with a sigh and begins to sing again with a soft melody reminiscent of a funeral rite. She adjusts her dress and calms her wavy and vibrant hair to show off the diadem she has worn throughout the battle.

"You're no ruler, and your crown has no power," says the king in a scared yet restrained tone.

"I prefer to think of it as an accessory," smirks Atansha in her melodic voice, "as my power comes from the earth spirits rather than a crown. A power like mine doesn't need oppressive castles or shiny jewelry, and I welcome any who would challenge a mortal who has made herself a deity. Your challenge was appointed to you and this is the moment of your failure."

"You can't do this! I am your king!" The man shrieks as he wrestles against the vines which tighten against his body and harden into stone.

"I have decided on the certainty of your death, and will not revisit it," says Atansha as she crushes the stone vines and the king with them.

"I will take over the kingdom now, and any in this room who prefer your king may join him," says Atansha while removing the vines from the soldiers and exiting the room with no concerns about being attacked by the angry men.

She bids the soldiers to fix the damage she caused and to restore the gardeners to the city, as there will soon be much more greenery that needs tending. The royal crier arrives at her demand and is told to announce her coronation in a few days. Atansha leaves to wait in her new chambers and prepare for the ceremony by performing a complex healing ritual for both the citizens and the lands of the kingdom.

General of the Winds

Diplomacy

"They're all dead, you know. Even if they survive the next fight they're only mortals," says a slender man with golden skin and cat-like facial features lying in repose on a gilded chaise. The man feasts on cheeses and fruit to pair with his crimson red wine. His eyes contain a purple sunburst iris centered around a slit pupil. He wears a long cloak made of blue velvet and a crisp white shirt, a perfect match to the elegance of the domed chamber around him.

"Oh don't be so negative, some may survive," chuckles a woman tapping her long fingers on a marble tabletop resting on top of a small cloud. Her hair is crisp and blonde with fine strands, and her face is as light as marble and glows brighter than the white dress that flows across her slender body.

"Our friend here does love them, after all. Sorry, I mean the General," she says while gesturing to a man in ornate armor sitting by the window with a pensive look on his face. The view from the window is mostly clouds, as to be expected at this altitude, yet his unwavering stare is fixed on something in particular.

"Good point, I tend to forget he is a mortal. Well, sort of anyway," says the purple cat man.

"Quiet, both of you," says the armored man sharply. "A room full of Royalty and I'm the only one you focus on?" His arm gestures across the room, which is filled with beings of all sorts. Some are more human than others, yet all share a bright glow around them and a smugness to their smiles as if they truly have achieved a carefree life.

Down at ground level, amidst the snow flurries and ice patches, an army approaches with the intent to siege the castle. The sound of drums shakes the high-walled castle and dissipates some of the neighboring low-hanging clouds as the nomadic warriors approach. The nomads are known for intimidation techniques and drawn-out sieges, a reputation in line with the sigil on their banners and shields—one of their warriors bludgeoning an enemy with a massive warhammer. It will take more than fear and hammers to invade the cloud castle, but their appearance certainly causes a stir among its inhabitants.

"Oh goody, a show to accompany dinner. I do love that these mortals believe we need their help," says the cat man with a grin.

"There are too many, the weapons won't last! I know they haven't learned from the previous battles," says the General. "We've got to help them—"

"Enough!" Boasts a rotund bearded man at the other end of the room. "The battle has begun, take your seats or take your leave."

The General flees the room in a hurry towards the nearest

staircase, so fast that he leaves a gust of wind in his wake that spills wine on the cat man's face. He's headed straight for the soldiers on the wall.

Though the castle's fortifications are thick and more than hundreds of feet tall, the approaching rhythmic doom is enough to send a panic through the newer members of the defending army. The novice soldiers in the castle are protected by a thick jacket with thin steel plates over their chest and shoulders and a quickly forged kettle hat helmet that can hardly survive a single blow. Their weapons are flimsy spears barely held together by a loose lashing and accompanied by what could be called a shield if one used their imagination. Two soldiers at the wall look down at the approaching army while trying to muster bravery, or at least enough focus to stay alive.

"I heard they celebrate victories by taking the dead from the battlefield and eating them," a shivering soldier mutters to his neighbor.

"Oh fuck off," says the neighbor. "You keep talking like that and you're sure to piss yourself, and I'll kill you if you get my boots wet."

"It's true. Some of the best weapons in the world too. Absolute castle destroyers."

"Soldiers! Eyes open and mouth closed or it's back to the gutter I pulled you from," shouts the older, lanky squad leader from far away as he snacks on an awkwardly juicy apple.

"I'm not buying it. I've seen them bury their dead," says a booming voice from behind them.

"Seen them? Yeah right! They haven't fought on this

continent in over a century. No one in this country is still alive who's seen them fight. Cannibals, all of them I say," retorts the shiverer from between his clacking teeth as he turns to face the new conversationalist.

The man behind them is immediately impressive and authoritative, his mid-length braided hair still rustled from his helmet and umber skin darkened further by time spent in the sun training the troops. His golden eyes are stern and sharp, a match to his boxy nose and strong jaw which has toughened up from years of bare knuckle fighting for sport. His flawless armor is ornate and perfectly articulated at every possible point of motion. He cracks a smile in anticipation of a duel of words and his aura is so powerful it gives off a golden glow that illuminates his body and shiny armor.

"Right..." says the glowing newcomer. "Well, if they have a victory to celebrate today it won't matter how they choose to mutilate your corpse. Best to focus on your training and stay alert to your enemies' movements."

He shoots a glance at the untrained and poorly equipped men in front of him, which reminds him of the original reason for his visit. The ragged fighters resemble the younger, more eager soldier he used to be and he hopes that they make it out of the battle alive.

"Uh, General! My apologies. I didn't know it was you, your highness," stutters the soldier while backpedaling his words and attempting a bow.

"Highness is for royalty, as is bowing," chuckles the General while putting his hand up to ask the soldier to save everyone the embarrassment.

"Right, your grace," blurts the soldier.

"Grace is for kings, and soldiers on the battlefield."

"I'm sorry, I'm not sure what to call you, sir. Perhaps you could help—".

"I'll help by ending this conversation here so I don't have to suffer through your attempts to showcase a vocabulary," interrupts the General as he walks away to find the squad leader.

"You miserable fool," says the annoyed neighbor as soon as the General is out of earshot. "General Yuudil has lived for centuries and would have seen the enemy in action. His power is known throughout the continent. Some say he's named after the sound of the breeze that flows through the plains. Others say it is the breeze that says his name as a show of respect."

General Yuudil finds the squad leader sitting on a chair well away from the wall.

"I trust you made the weapon improvements I suggested, squad leader," says the General with an inquisitive tone.

"The spears are fine," the leader says dismissively. "They're invulnerable, like my men." Now with a hint of arrogance.

"Right. Good to know," says the General as he grabs a spear from a stack of spares.

He begins to spin the spear as if tracing a sphere around himself while moving his feet in a dance and muttering repeatedly in a foreign tongue.

"*Fereh diche unkipe, unkipe oonkala.*" A swirling tornado surrounds him for a split second then dissipates.

General of the Winds

He casually leaps off the wall and falls hundreds of feet into a group of two dozen adversaries. He lands on his feet with a force that shakes the earth and a burst of air that knocks back the closest opposing troops, crushing them against the stone wall instantly. Even a battlefield covered in ice and snow is no match for Yuudil's graceful power. The armored warrior whips the spear around, tripping enemies before stabbing them, wrestling swords away from others, and long-reach sword fighting.

The spear makes contact with its first shield and crumbles with such little resistance that it negates all the strength behind the swing. The General is now unarmed and surrounded by enemy troops with no hope of support from his archers. The troops on the wall gasp and panic as they try to plan how to save him without getting themselves killed. Reinforcements from the nomadic army are approaching quickly, so there isn't much time.

The General lets out a heavy sigh and shakes his head as he unsheathes a massive glowing sword from his back that is far too large to have been stored in his armor. In another effortless and mechanical act, he lays waste to the remaining soldiers. He spins his sword so fast that it tears up dirt and plants behind him, then leaps up hundreds of feet to land back on the wall.

"How about now you fix the spears," he says as he tosses the broken spear at the feet of the amazed infantry leader. His tossing motion ends with an aggressive point at the shocked man that seems to cut through all the leader's armor and through to his insecurities.

"The spears will be fine if the wielders know how to use

them," the infantry leader says with a cheeky smirk as he hides his amazement.

An equally cheeky and self-amused grin comes over the General's face before he grabs another spear from a soldier, tripping three of them with one swipe, kicking another into the high side of the wall, and disarming the last soldier. Then, he throws the leader against the wall and lets the spear swing out to graze the edge of the man's neck.

"It appears I use the spear just fine," the General says with a chuckle. "If I can't even defend myself with these sticks then what hope do you have for this untrained rabble you hauled up from the street in chains last week? Fix, the fucking, spears." The General gestures to the tower he came from. "The Royals demand my attention now, see that you don't require any more of mine."

He drops the spear and walks away hastily, paying no attention to the angry looks from some of the men nor the glare from the embarrassed infantry leader. He didn't miss the looks of those who enjoyed watching the prick get what he deserved, nor was the increase of morale lost on the one who was willing to jump alone into the battle to help the cause.

"Fix the spears!!!!" Bemoans the leader in a screechy tone.

Born of Flame

Saboteur

A large army clothed in white, gold, and purple parades through a prairie after their victory in battle over a younger neighboring nation. The younger nation was born from a successful rebellion and has been amassing territory at a rapid rate—completing the cycle of revolutionaries turned tyrants.

The army's bards sing songs of triumph that echo for miles, and the soldiers' unified footsteps shake the ground with a terrifying rhythm. Cavalry officers flaunt banners bearing the regal colors as they make their rounds through the squadrons to ensure no soldiers fall out of line. The formation shifts from hundreds of soldiers wide to a single squadron abreast as they approach a narrow gap through the mountains carved by an ancient river.

A lone figure stands at the mouth of the river valley in front of them, blocking the king's massive army from returning home. The shadowy figure is wearing a hooded cloak that appears to have survived many fires and channeled the energy from those fires into an ominous orange glow.

The figure's reddish cloak covers most of his face, and what skin can be seen is so thin it is hardly distinguishable from the actual bone. The light around the figure begins to sizzle, as if the air itself is heating up, and turns into thick dark smoke.

A cavalry knight donning fashionable armor patterned with the colors of his king rides with his squadron to tell the figure to leave. The horses rear up to show their discomfort with the shadow man but the soldiers reign them in and force them to proceed.

"You must move aside for the king and his convoy," warns the knight. Even the plumage on his helmet moves with arrogance.

The cloaked figure makes no attempts to move away from the army and instead continues muttering to himself in a tongue unknown to even the most knowledgeable scribes of the kingdom. He moves his arms in a strange motion, something akin to a slow dance, as if reacting to invisible actors around him.

"If you don't leave we will be forced to attack," bellows the knight in a lackluster fashion.

"Good," says the shadow beneath the cloak as he whips his head around to face the knight with an unwavering dead-eye stare. The figure is still as stone as he stares at the knight.

"Leave now," snaps the knight with a slight crackle in his voice, "while the king allows it, or bow before his might to beg for mercy."

"Gods don't bow to kings," says the figure as he cracks a smile showing teeth that don't quite look human.

The hood over the figure begins to glow with firelight as if the eyes of the stranger were filled with the flames of the sun in the sky above. As the knight feels sweat pool across his brow, he senses he is the target of an evil incantation.

The hooded stranger races to the knight's horse with incomprehensible speed, leaving a trail of fire in his wake that sets nearby troops ablaze. He throws the knight off his horse and shouts an incantation that sends a bubbling flame into his face, causing his body to ignite while he screams. When the burning eventually stops, the knight still lives—if it can be described as life. His armor has become molten and glows red hot, his skin is charred and seems to bubble like a layer of thin rock resting delicately above a lake. Smoke clouds his body as the flesh beneath becomes ash, leaving a mostly incorporeal mass in its place. The knight stands still while other troops attempt to attack the magick wielder, a god he must be, though such things are thought to be no more than myths spread by the bards.

The sorcerer god slays each soldier who charges him, the way one flips through paper stacks to sort them. He throws soldiers hundreds of feet away and sets others ablaze, yet the fire comes from his hands now and requires less of his focus. After a few dozen are chosen, the deity scans the battlefield and shouts fireballs at six more mounted knights, converting them into six more flaming thrall knights. The weapons of all seven knights transform into long spellcasting staffs paired with a broadsword.

The fire god then starts chanting in the same unfamiliar language and raises his hands to the heavens, stomps his foot, and sends a shockwave of heated air and rubble through the entire front half of the army. From the cracks in the ground made by the stomp, a bubbling flame engulfs all it reaches, thus completing the recruitment. The stranger snaps his fingers and commands his newly transformed troops to turn around, and around they turn, to form a new line against their own countrymen. The god's pyroclastic flow dissipates and the real battle has begun.

Controlled by sorcery, the infernal army pushes forward belligerently, like a sharpened chisel tearing through soft wood, with no regard for tactics or defense against counterattacks. The smoke and flames under the molten armor don't leave much for steel to contact, and any flesh remaining can be lost without impairing the movement of the chthonic beasts. This wedge-shaped blaze pushes towards its sole target, the royal caravan. As the bodies pile up along the wedge's path, the volcanic knights speed over the carcasses and select those who can be reborn from flame. Those selected are grabbed by lava flows breaking through the earth to begin their transformation.

The heated horde breaks through to the king and continues onward to keep the opponents far away, as the burning rabble stands no chance against the invincible shield of protection summoned around the royalty. The molten knights do not follow. Instead, they attack and slaughter the king's guard, save for the one whom they could not best. Tumboldt, personal bodyguard to the king and one they say could crush a man, armor and all, without a weapon. The royal guardian digs his flail deep into the heart of one of the horses, sending the flaming knight to the ground. As he raises his weapon to deliver a killing blow, the fire god breaks concentration for the first time in the battle and flies across the battlefield to smash Tumboldt into a nearby rock. Tumboldt manages to get to his feet and sees that the knights are attempting to break the magickal shield protecting his king, though he can not help as he knows the god before him means to end him.

Just as he turns to scan for his attacker, he is pushed to the ground and a scorching hot dagger is thrust into his side. He begins to feel himself heating up across his whole body, soon to become one of the wretched slaves of this sorcerer. As he feels himself turning, he sees a bright light shining from the heavens and feels his body go cold as ice. Not painful like frostbite, but refreshing like iced tea after a day in the sun. Nay, today will not see Tumboldt the Guardian become a thrall for this servant of an unknown demon. He thrusts the knife from his side and uses the power of the light to throw the deity onto his back. They both stand up and pause to see what the other will do as they catch their breath.

"Tumboldt the Unturnable, impressive," says the fire god with a look of amusement. "If you leave now, the halls of your homeland will sing tales of your valor and your name will live forever. You have proven yourself formidable and worthy of life after today. Go now, while I allow it."

He stands there watching Tumboldt's anguish as if he feeds off the fear and grief spreading through his enemy.

Tumboldt feels the blood pouring down his side and sees the corrupted knights casting an enchantment to bring down the king's shield. From behind the shield, he hears insults and half-hearted attempts from the royals to bully him into saving the king. He pays them no heed, for they will never leave the valley. Even though the king is despicable and has never cared about anyone but himself, Tumboldt feels an unexplainable drive to maintain his oaths and see this foe vanquished.

With the wounds sustained and the power of this unknown foe, Tumboldt knows he will never see another sunrise. He remembers a saying from one of the elders in his city, "The only parts of us that live forever are the stories told by those we leave behind." But Tumboldt's longest living story is the one that doesn't make it back to his family. The story that begins in this very moment.

He says goodbye to his family, begs their forgiveness for leaving them, and prays that this evil will not find its way to them. He prays to his gods that he can earn a legacy worth telling, even if all he can do is slow down this vicious hell beast. He is filled with fears of his village burning and the suffering of good people at the hand of this madman, the loss of all he knows in this world because of his inaction. He watches paralyzed as the royal shield comes down in a dazzling show of sparks and the retreat of something like a tent made of colorful liquid.

As the shield goes down, the king is the first to die. But he is just a trophy, as the real target is the source of the magick shield, the wizard of the realm. Drained from the energy spent on the shield, he barely puts up a fight as the angry god drains his life force, his Will, from his body.

Born of Flame

When the soul theft is complete, the ground shakes as a torrent of lava and fire springs out from all around the army of arson. Soldiers from all sides begin to lift from the ground caught in a tornado of flames, bodies swirling and slamming into each other as they fuse into a single being. A colossal form emerges from the flames and takes the shape of a vicious demon, horned and winged and terrible—a shackled demon sent to an arcane prison by ancient powers forgotten by this world a millenia ago.

With no delusions of killing his foe, or even of his survival, Tumboldt lets out a battle shout in the tongue of his high priests and stands up tall to charge the sorcerer god with his flail in full swing. With both hands on the hilt, he builds up momentum in the chain and hurls the spiked ball with ferocity. He catches the deity in the back with a single spike, drawing a small amount of what should have been blood from the wound. The god throws Tumboldt off him, breaking his back and neck completely on impact.

As the demon gets closer to taking full form, the gash made by Tumboldt splits open and breaks the concentration of the spellcasting god. He howls as he feels pain for the first time since the neighboring mountains were carved by the river flowing on the edge of the battlefield.

The volcanic tornado collapses and explodes with tectonic energy, sending the spellcaster flying across the plain. He stands up, dusts himself off, and looks around to find Tumboldt's body.

In a voice that echoes with the thousands of souls this evil spellcaster has stolen through the years, he screeches "You have delayed my plans and for that, I shall curse your flesh so that your soul may never know peace! I eternally damn you and your descendants! I shall have what I am owed!"

The god begins a barbaric torture ritual but is stopped after only a few words by another beam of light from the sky that forms an unbreakable wall around the dying man.

A woman walks out of the beam of light, unbothered by the mounds of flaming carrion and the fire deity who made them. She places a tender hand on the broken body of the knight, leaving behind a mist of starlight and silver. She stands up and glares sternly at the god before her.

"Heed my words, a curse begets a curse. One of Tumboldt's line will bring about your demise at the peak of your power. Your life has been extended, but the promise made by the Sea Witch will be fulfilled."

The fire god shudders as a massive wave approaches from the nearby river. A woman with a large black hat walks on top of the wave. The wave glimmers various colors as the torrent collapses on Tumboldt and lifts his body. She steps off the wave onto dry land and the water recedes, with his body in tow, back into the river where a small dinghy awaits.

"See you soon." She smiles knowingly at the fire god and walks back to the boat casually.

Enraged by the slight, he flees from the encounter to continue his plan. He severs the head of the king to place it in a small jar next to the heads of other kings and nobles stored in his cloak.

Born of Flame

The triumphant god walks away to where the bodies are amassed and picks up a few crimson crystals which sparkle and glow with light red veins running through the crystal.

"Right, off to the next then," he sighs.

The sorcerer god leaves the valley with great haste in search of another pile of bodies large enough to energize his patron.

Sea Witch

Psychopomp

A violent storm erupts out of nowhere in a small village too far from castles and lords to be claimed by any kingdom. Inside a small cottage near the inn, an old man lies down to sleep for the night. He kisses a painting of a woman next to a ring much too intricate to match the rest of the decorations, then tells her he will see her soon but not too soon. He is a bit restless but begins to drift off to sleep as he notices a figure approaching him slowly and with caution. He quickly tries to sit up but doesn't feel the sensation of moving, though he seems to be sitting up based on his viewpoint.

The figure emerges from the shadows to reveal a woman, tall and slender with fawn white skin that reminds him of sea salt and beaches. On her head sits a large, round black hat with a wide brim that extends well beyond her shoulders and is topped with white flowers. Her face is stern but gentle, with a soft smile masking the turbulence building beneath the surface. She wears a white ruffled shirt under a black corset containing boning made of shells that reflect a cacophony of colors. Below the corset is a black skirt that hangs in a wide bell shape and almost touches the ground. She is grounded by a pair of thick heeled boots that are battered by years spent in saltwater.

"Hey Wren," she says tenderly while reaching out her arm towards his. "Let me show you something."

"I'd rather go back to sleep. I'm tired," he moans while lying back down and covering his face.

"You *are* asleep, Wren, in a manner of speaking," she says with a sweeping gesture that points back at his body in his bed ten feet behind him.

"How did I get here?! What is this?!" He screams and backs away from the woman.

"All in time." She turns her palm up towards him to invite him to hold it while holding her dress up with the other hand.

She opens the door of his cabin as he cowers to shield himself from the thunderstorm he hears outside, but there is no rain in sight. There is no village either. Wren rubs his eyes and looks between the outside and inside in an attempt to comprehend how everything keeps moving. The view through the door is of a beautiful beach marking the end of a turbulent ocean full of magickal water just as colorful and vibrant as the shells on her corset. The sun is setting over the water, and as Wren watches its reflection dance across the waves he feels a sense of welcoming and warmth from the otherworldly water. The smell of saltwater floods his nose, a welcome change from the musty cabin and farming village he's used to.

As he steps out of his cabin, he looks back at it and sees a completely different building on the outside. It is a large white house with black trim and vines growing up the side paneling.

Wren feels it would be scary at night but is very appealing in the evening sun.

"Where's my village?" He says frantically as tears roll down his face.

"Where you left it."

"Where's my body?"

"Same answer."

"What is this place?"

She pauses for a second, looks at the ground, then looks at him with a weak but genuine smile.

"Your new home."

The Witch places a gentle hand on his shoulder and points him towards the water's edge where the waves crash against each other with terrifying ferocity. He catches a glimpse of a large ship on the horizon and feels both fear and curiosity rising from his gut. She turns and begins to walk away but pauses as he speaks.

"I'm going back home, you go ahead," he mumbles.

"There's no going back now, I'm afraid," she says sternly.

"Will I be ok?" He asks timidly.

"Yes."

"What if there is nothing for me there?"

"I didn't realize *she* was nothing to you," says the Witch with a slight grin and a twinkle in her eye.

"Ok, I'll go." He nods vigorously in agreement and begins to follow her.

As she walks into the violent ocean, the water begins to fly from her presence, forming equally massive waves that crash into the original ones. The freshly exposed sand retains the golden reflection of the setting sun atop the rainbow glow of the water around it. At the end of the newly made beach, a small dinghy pops up from beneath the waves. The seaweed and barnacle-covered boat remains motionless as if it awaits their arrival. Wren and the Witch climb into the dinghy and take a seat.

Creatures appear from the water around and begin to circle the boat to hitch themselves to it. The beings look like sea dragons, with long flowing tendrils coming off their bodies and a saddle of sorts on their back. The color of the dragons is hard for Wren to pin down due to their spectral appearance and the rippling of the waves around them. They begin pulling the dinghy in the direction of a larger ship in the distance.

The dinghy continues towards the distant ship, enjoying the calm waters created for it by the water creatures. A thick, smokey fog surrounds the ship, making it hard to discern any details from a distance. As he approaches the ship, Wren notices it is a large, old galleon seemingly devoid of a crew and passengers. The only way onto the ship is a decrepit rope ladder that can hardly hold itself up, much less the weight of a slow-moving old man. Wren's mind toils as he tries to think of how he can make it onto this terrifying ship. Just as he is about to make his concerns known, the ship rocks in a massive wave and leans towards the dinghy, allowing it to ride the wave right onto the deck.

Wren steps carefully off the dinghy, thankful for the more stable deck, and the Witch walks slowly to the bow of the ship.

Suddenly, a second wave crashes over the bow and the whole ship goes underwater. Wren can feel himself floating just above the deck, yet somehow he isn't drowning. As he gains his composure, he gazes at the myriad of sea creatures around him. He notices that the ship is next to a cliff overlooking an ocean trench fifty feet below the surface. The light has somewhat disappeared, except for the aura surrounding the Sea Witch.

A pod of dolphins plays on the water's surface high above the masts, fifty grey animals clicking and whistling as they crash through the waves. A gargantuan whale swims up from the depths with an eye taller than Wren and a mouth large enough to swallow the ship. Blue sharks sneak along the cliff side with fins that drag like curtains, and shoals of fish swarm the deck, which swirl around the Witch and narrowly avoid hitting Wren. Massive tentacles emerge from the depths to pick at the shoals and pay no notice to Wren.

The polyps and anemones stuck to the ship come alive to form a vibrant coral reef on the ship, which makes Wren feel he's been transported to another world. The dreamlike glow of the coral, combined with their strange movements, add to Wren's feeling of awe at the magick around him.

The sea dragons that pulled the dinghy to the ship join the frenzy. Wren is able to see them clearly now, each one is a mass of kelp-like tendrils joined to a tubular body that floats along in the current like a leaf in the breeze. Their rainbow glow is apparent, even underwater, and their transparent bodies almost meld into a single form.

At the center of the frenzy is the Witch, unmoved by the

water and its inhabitants. She begins to walk effortlessly towards Wren, as if she were walking on land, with a large shell in her hand. The shell is covered in years of sea growth on the outside, but the inside is radiant and colorful and glows brilliantly. The Witch holds the shell with both hands and brings it to Wren's face as if to offer him a drink of the water already surrounding him. As he grabs the shell and drinks in its contents, he can feel the spirit of the ocean entering his body. The love of the ocean heals his worried heart and calms his emotions.

The ship surfaces and Wren lands on the deck soaked and covered in sea life. The Witch, however, is completely dry and clean. She walks to the helm, pulls out a spyglass, and steers the ship towards some unknown destination.

"Welcome, Wren," she says, "to the Mighty Dead. It's a long journey across the sea to meet the others, but you'll be with your lover soon enough. I suggest you get some rest now."

Wren nods and heads below deck, his mind racing with curiosity about what the other side could hold.

Shy Not

Look to yourself for the meaning of life.
For though all lives share the same material composition,
Each meaning is unique.
Like a fingerprint for the soul.
Trouble is,
Much like a new employee knows not their tasks,
Your soul may not yet know its purpose.
Thus, exploration is needed.
Shy not from the things that move you,
For they move you towards your purpose.

Celestial Mother

In the middle of the night, at the top of a mountain peeking out above a restless forest, a woman gazes at the surrounding vista frustrated at her inability to recreate its beauty. She sits on a large boulder that she uses as a makeshift desk. Her porcelain skin shines in the moonlight and her blonde hair is pulled up into a messy bun. Broken pencils and crumpled papers litter the rock's surface, showcasing her many attempts to create a landscape drawing that's up to her standards.

Partly distracted and partly hoping for inspiration, she abandons her drawing and turns her attention upwards to the clear night sky. In her most inspired act of the night, she decides to draw the sky above her. She holds a sheet of paper firm against the rock face while she sketches as fast as she can. Her pencil flies across the paper as she glances between the sky and her hurried recreation.

Nebulas and constellations fill the page until she notices that one celestial body, a nebula shaped like a wolf, is far from where it should be. She begins a new drawing and maps the location of the constellation, but notices it has shifted again before she can draw it fully. This second error stirs a sense of curiosity in her as she tries to understand it.

The amateur stargazer flips through her drawings from the

night and notices that this nebula has drifted all over the sky, and not in the same direction as the other celestials. As she pauses to comprehend the anomaly, a beam of multicolored light shines down from the nebula onto her paper. Once the light dissipates, the wolf nebula she drew begins to move around the page in a lively and animated manner. The lines of the wolf boil and wiggle as it moves, then the wolf leaps out of the page and takes on a full three-dimensional form.

The wolf glows a wide range of hues and its form defies logic, as it appears to be a solid shape composed of amorphous fog and pure light. The wolf pays no attention to the woman, leading her to wonder if the wolf appeared to inspire her or simply as a random manifestation of energy.

Chaotic masses of raw creation fall behind the wolf as it dashes along the mountaintop. The masses are inexplicable shapes that bubble and transform from one curiosity to the next, as if evolving to match their surroundings. Eventually, each mass stops transforming and solid shapes emerge, but the form is different for each entity. Among the chaos of creation, two rocks form, a pencil for the star recorder, and even a bunny rabbit is born from nothing.

The woman is in a state of shock and awe during the whole event but works up the courage to say something just as the wolf turns back into a beam of light and disappears abruptly.

She collects her thoughts and drawing tools then examines the world around her again, but this time with a newfound fascination for the heavens and what they contain. Her newly created pencil becomes an extension of herself as intuition guides her creations. She obsessively creates endless sketches, all of which are the best she's ever made. She will carry this newly birthed imagination with her everywhere she goes, but decides to return to this rock when that creativity is in need of nurturing.

Chthonic Father

Fear

King Arundel sits on sumptuous sheets and pillows strewn across a supersized stone bed. His ruffled raven hair rests against his smooth golden sepia skin and sharp cheeks. He lies among his lot of lustful lovers, pleading they provide him plump berries and port wine. He partakes in peaceful puffs of his pipe, filled with the finest flowers of the Three Staves. His bare body is barricaded behind thin robes bolstered by a belt and baldric tied fast across his shoulder, both weaved with a voluptuous velvet. His naked knees nuzzle against his nearest neighbor, their skin touching and their hips pressed together.

An erratic emotion erupts that ends his ecstasy and causes him to look out over the sea beyond his bed to behold the beauty of the sunset. Patches of blues, yellows, and purples blanket the skies and dance across the gentle waves beneath. The ports are filled with merchant ships in various stages of their journeys to flood markets with goods and feed the royal coffers. A disagreement on the docks catches Arundel's attention, crime is common among the working class but he's never paid attention to it before today. A tinge of guilt comes over him as he thinks about the desperation of the peasants who barely have enough to survive.

His round brown eyes stray to another sight seen from his open-air colonnade high on the hill, to the smithing region responsible for crafting the goods aboard the merchant ships. The houses are of a craft far beneath that of the products created within and have only decayed with time. Their broken roofs and muddy streets make the slums easily distinguishable from the immaculate neighborhoods the king feels safe visiting. He wonders what life is like for his subjects, then focuses on how strange the thought is and briefly fears how they view him.

The king is pulled from his pensive position as he perceives himself being leaned backwards and his bulging baldric unbuttoned. The stone slab is so soft and soothing that he starts to snooze slowly as pairs of hands and plump lips peruse his person. Drunken curiosities turn into chaotic dreams as his consciousness dissipates.

He awakes in a dream, next to a lake surrounded by an inviting and richly green forest. The slow rippling water reflects the trees beyond it and that reflection quickly grows fuzzier as a rainstorm sweeps in. The rain continues and the temperature drops quickly, turning the rain into sleet and sleet into snow. The trees across the lake change color and drop their leaves. The fallen leaves decompose and the lake dries up revealing a stone tunnel covered in moss that leads further underground.

As he approaches the tunnel he smells the death around him before he sees it. The tunnel is covered in moss, fungus, and a variety of bugs. He doesn't want to go in but feels an alluring sense of fear and curiosity forcing him to do so. He slowly makes his way through the tunnel and finds a large stone sepulcher full of more death recyclers and other unsightly creatures. The chamber reeks of death but is crawling with life, the kind of life that survives by scavenging and returning energy from corpses back to the living.

The rock forming the ceiling has been eroded by moisture, leaving stalactites hanging all around the room. A small group of bats clings to the last bit of shadow that remains untouched by the light from the doorway.

As he becomes more comfortable in the space, he notices a sarcophagus with a body inside of it. He edges closer and realizes that the body is his own, but he knows he isn't dead. He can't be. As he bumps into a large figure behind him, the room gets darker and colder immediately and a visceral fear returns to him. His stomach turns, his body freezes, and his eyes close uncontrollably. His heart beats so fast that it seems to not beat at all. He hears a deep, growling voice speak from behind him.

"No, you are not dead. I assume you've concluded that already. You can think of this encounter as a dream, a vision, or simply as a memento mori—a reminder of your eventual death."

He turns around to face the disembodied voice and is met with the strangest creature he's ever seen. Its form is fluid and smokey, but what remains constant is the form of a black cat-like creature far taller than him. Emerging from the smokey form of this creature he can see more moss, mycelium, and insects, which leads the king to question whether it is covered in detritus or whether the detritus grows from the creature itself.

Chthonic Father

"What, what are you?" He asks timidly—a state in which this pampered king rarely finds himself.

"I am known by some as the Chthonic Father, a spirit embodying the forces that work to replenish life by repurposing that which dies and decays."

"Bugs and death. Gross," he scoffs.

"Yes, we are often scorned and feared by those who refuse all thoughts of death and those who wrongly assume we bring death. Death, however, is inseparable from life and thus its Will is tied to life. We merely continue the cycle by allowing new life to form where death strikes, giving meaning to the life that was lost. You can look to us as a way to repurpose your deepest fears into a passion for life and use the inevitability of death as a way to create meaning for that same life, or you can squander the finite amount of time you have left. Your life is your own, as are the choices you make during it. Ask yourself if you are the king you want to be, and if that is the same king your subjects want you to be."

The creature vanishes into the shadows, leaving the man alone and in shock. He wakes immediately, flustered and disoriented, burdened by fears of failing to be a ruler worthy of the legacy he desires. He resumes his hedonistic consumption but is plagued with thoughts of how he can improve the lives of those in squalor. He takes note of others who would oppose his changes—especially those who use violence to maintain their authority. He reluctantly plans a renovation of the docks to provide safe storage away from thieves and a massive overhaul of the slums across the kingdom. His changes may not all be perfect, but he confidently chooses action over wavering indecision.

The full moon rises high in the sky above him, and those around him have fallen fast asleep. His plans reach a point of cohesion and plausibility, leading him to feel comfortable pausing for the night. He pulls his bedmates closer and drifts off to sleep again, but this time is filled with thoughts of how he can help his kingdom prosper.

Book Two

The Present

A look at the present day as it is.
Where crowns have become corporations, rationality has
been deified, and magick has been replaced by science.
Or so we're told...

Binky

On a planet similar to Earth, at an airport near the ocean, passengers scurry around the terminals trying to make their flights. The departure area is gridlocked and a cacophony of car horns fills the outside air. The golden glow of the fall evening sun covers the edges of the landscape and the buildings in a wonderful filigree.

Inside the terminal, a woman in her late twenties arrives at her gate early to wait for her flight. She is short and lean, but made taller by her high heels, and is towing a large carry-on suitcase with an animal carrier on top. Her designer luggage shines a bright white that blends into her white pantsuit and matching beret. Her large, round sunglasses cover her tired eyes.

She sits down in an empty seat and immediately meets eyes with a large stone statue across from her. The statue is a memorial to a knight who fought against a dragon centuries ago and was victorious. The knight holds his shield against his body to protect himself from the dragon's jaws while attacking the serpent's eye with a long sword. Alas, the dragon is preparing for the fire breath that would end the knight's life. The plaque at the bottom of the statue speaks about the knight's life and praises his bravery.

"What a weird statue to put here, Binky," says the woman while patting the small pet carrier in the seat next to her. "Don't they know people bring their babies here?"

The woman pulls her baby out of the carrier to kiss and pet it. The baby is a small, fuzzy white dragon that weighs about twenty pounds and breathes heavily out of excitement for his human's attention. Binky has a tongue too long for his mouth and a very asymmetrical face.

"I know you'd never hurt anyone, Binky." The woman baby-talks to the dragon and kisses him all over his face. "Why do people think all dragons are so big and scary? Humans haven't even seen anything bigger than a horse in decades and dragon attacks are less common than other pet species. Who could be scared of this *cute wittle face*?"

Binky's face squishes and squashes as she tugs on it, and his wall-eyed smile removes any doubts that this creature is capable of causing harm. She pulls him in for a tight hug.

Other passengers with small dragons and other pets roam around the airport as the sun sets. Dogs and cats are also common pets, but dragons have become popular as a hypoallergenic option for the "purse dog" crowd. Dragons that small rarely have any breath attacks and their long life spans make them a good fit for pet lovers. They tend to get along with mammals and other magickal creatures if socialized properly.

The woman stares out the window at the moon, which is partially obscured by fog and clouds. A small commercial plane operated by Meersh Airlines takes off overhead, cutting between the clouds. A powerful lightning strike lights up a massive dragon silhouette easily five times larger than the plane. As the flash dissipates, red lights begin blinking and a siren is heard.

"What the fuck?!" Shouts the woman as she looks around to see if other passengers know what is happening.

Several other passengers stand in awe and three others run off immediately. A red flash of flames as bright as the sun lights up the clouds, revealing the landscape around the terminal like a pseudo-daylight. Bodies and objects from the recently destroyed plane begin falling onto the airport and people around it. Everyone begins to evacuate the airport in a very disorderly fashion, including the woman and her pet dragon.

"Oh shit, Binky. Let's go!" She says while packing up their belongings. "Ok, I've got your water bowl, your toys, my tablet and my headphones. I'm not sitting around to find out what the hell that noise is outside."

She gently places Binky in his carrier and runs to join the fleeing mob making their way to the doors. People are shouting and pushing, but the woman stays steady and works her way through the crowd with Binky safely in tow.

As she exits the building, tornado-force winds from the dragon's massive wings knock her over and send people and cars flying across the street. She gathers her footing and hides behind a thick wall of concrete nearby.

Then, an earthquake hits as the giant beast lands and cracks the ground beneath it. The dragon begins melting airplanes with a flame breath so hot the woman can feel herself sweating. The steel beams making up the building's skeleton begin to crumble under the immense heat. The dragon lets out a roar to claim dominance over the area and begins searching for more victims. Each step shakes the entire airport, exacerbating the existing damage and sending some folks running for safer cover. The woman holds her breath to keep from making noise and signals Binky to keep quiet.

She peeks her head around the wall to get a better look at the beast and is in utter shock.

"Damn, Binky," she whispers. "This is the type of dragon people are expecting when I tell them about you. It's gotta be bigger than a football field."

Binky lets out a sigh of agreement. The dragon's head is a deep shade of red and covered in thick scales that form an intricate pattern. Its angry eyes are bright yellow with a slit pupil that darts around as it takes in its surroundings. The spikes sticking out from the scales are a clean ivory color, and two large black horns stick out of the rear part of its skull. Its front foot is larger than the airport bus crushed beneath it and has gargantuan talons like a bird of prey.

A tense silence fills the air as survivors hide and the dragon lifts its head to get a better sniff. The dragon senses Binky's presence and turns its head straight towards the shattered concrete wall protecting Binky and his owner. The woman panics and begins looking for a hiding spot that can withstand the heat of the dragon's breath. The dragon aims its body at the crumbling wall protecting his adversary and draws a deep breath in to ready an attack.

Suddenly, the beast is launched into the air as if the earth itself returned the force of the violent landing. Large pillars of dirt rise from the ground at incredible speeds but don't cause much damage outside of the area containing the dragon.

The enormous dragon is juggled by mountain-sized pillars erupting out of the ground each time it touches down. It is pushed to the seashore miles away and onto a patch of sand that dries up as the dragon approaches. The wave made by the sudden shift of waters crashes over the massive beast, drowning it momentarily, and continues onward to flood the nearby area containing the airport.

The cowering crowd flees to a tall hill in search of dry land and a safe spot from which to watch the event. The woman helps with crowd control and directs the more confused people to safety.

"Over there!" She shouts and points at a watchtower on the hilltop. "There's a building where we can stay dry and try to find out what's happening."

She leads the crowd up the hill and onto the concrete platform holding the watchtower. Once the last person is through she climbs onto an elevated section of the structure and sets Binky down next to her.

Back in the ocean, the fire breather shakes off the attack and attempts to take flight but is knocked out of the sky by sudden and violent winds. Just as it begins to recover, it is tackled by a slightly smaller yellowish dragon with four wings that emerges from the clouds. The yellow dragon is still more massive than any other dragon known to exist and is far more nimble in the air than its fire-breathing adversary. This new dragon seems incapable of breathing fire but its four long wings are used to produce gusts of air powerful enough to combat the scorching flames.

The two dragons are equally matched and their stalemate brings a short pause to the intense fight. The yellow air dragon screeches at the fire breather as if it were offering a chance to surrender. The fire breather roars back and catches the yellow dragon off guard with a breath attack, sending it flying backwards. The aggressor prepares for a larger attack against its foe.

From the depths of the sea, a water beast emerges that is so large its tentacles are nearly as thick as the fire breather's entire body. The red dragon is grappled by the purple tentacles and thrown to the ground so forcibly that the onlookers feel the ground shake from miles away. The dragon's fiery skin sizzles and steams as it is held in the water, causing it to let out a cry of pain. The red dragon stops fighting and goes silent as it admits defeat.

The large water beast releases its hold on the dragon and its tentacle makes another massive wave as it goes underwater. Further out to sea, an eye emerges from the depths that is larger than either dragon and is fixed on the fire spirit. The eye blinks slowly and a deep growl emanates from beneath the waves.

The fire dragon slowly rises and bows to the two foes, gestures to the ground beneath it as well, then holds the pose as a sign of resignation. Once satisfied that the destruction is over, the water and air beasts depart and leave the wounded leviathan to tend to itself. The red dragon limps forward to gain speed and manages to take flight. It ascends into the clouds and vanishes.

The woman and those around her breathe a sigh of relief as they look around at the total destruction of the airport and the surrounding buildings. Most of the water has receded into the ocean but the flooding has left pools of water in some of the wreckage. The airport is demolished. The air traffic control tower has fallen onto one of the hangers, causing an explosion that went unnoticed during the fight. The few functioning sirens are blasting and the lights attached to them are flashing.

A crew of emergency personnel has already arrived to care for the survivors and assess the damage. They've roped off an area free of debris to set up a makeshift base and are herding the injured towards the medical tents.

"That was insane, Binky," says the woman. "I bet no one has ever seen anything like that before! They were so big! We almost died multiple times! Ughhh, I'm not gonna get out of this city now. Shit."

The woman flips off the dragon and sneers at it before making her way back to the unfunctional airport to meet with the recently arrived emergency personnel. As her adrenaline wears off, she begins to comprehend the reality of the situation and is grateful to be alive.

Embrace the Change

An old, blue sedan pulls off a windy mountain road to stop for snacks and beer for a weekend getaway. The driver, a tall man with shoulder-length curly blonde hair beneath his signature red trucker hat, steps out of the car along with a dense cloud of smoke. Another man, this one shorter with thick, dark hair and a metal concert t-shirt, is fast asleep in the passenger seat. From the backseat, a woman with blue highlights and white skin emerges with a large shepherd dog on a leash.

"Damn. The sign says no dogs, Tina," the tall man says while pointing at one of the many signs posted on the front door. "You stay out here with Sadie and I'll get the goods."

"Thanks, Quentin!" Tina walks her pup over to an empty bench near an old man smoking in a camping chair.

"I guess our buddy Mike passed out already," says Quentin with a chuckle as he walks inside the store. Mike shows no signs of waking from his slumber in the passenger seat.

The old man next to Tina smiles, revealing what is left of his teeth as he chews on his cigar and mutters a song to himself. "What brings a pair of pups like you this far into the woods?" His words whistle as he talks.

"Just hanging out," says Tina slowly with a reserved shrug. "We heard it should rain this weekend, that sounds kinda nice."

"Oh sure, it'll be raining cats and dogs up here—mostly dogs, I reckon. Full moon tonight too, if you didn't know already. You folks don't get much of the rain down in the city, do ya? It's drier than a sponge in the summer sun out there."

Tina chuckles, a nice break from the paranoia caused by the trace amounts of psilocybin in her system. She retorts, "Yeah, I guess that's a way to put it. It'll be nice to let Sadie here run around in the woods and breathe some fresh air for a change."

"Careful up in them woods, now. The critters get big out here, and you don't want anything to happen to lil' Ms. Sadie."

"Thanks, I'll keep an eye out," says Tina in a frustrated tone as her paranoia grows again inside her.

Meanwhile, inside the store, Quentin places three cases of craft beer and an armful of snacks on the register counter. The cashier behind the counter is another elderly man with a tight beard and an old ball cap to hide his bare head.

"Nice beer choice," says the cashier with a smile. "That's a lotta beer for one night, sir."

"Oh, we're here for the long weekend," says Quentin, confused about the stranger's judgement. "We've got another car meeting us at the cabin later."

"The whole weekend, eh? You're at the old Richardson's place off Walnut Street, ain't ya? No other rental cabins for miles."

"Uh, yep that sounds like the place."

"Do yourself a favor and don't do nothing dumb like climbing up on the roofs. Them spikes up there is hard as steel and they'll put a hole in you so big astronomers'll come to explore it. They ain't just for birds in these woods."

Quentin pauses to process whether he actually heard the man say this or whether the mushrooms in his bowels are out for revenge. He catches a glimpse of a large dog standing in an aisle before it vanishes.

"Right, no rooftop parties. Sounds easy enough! I thought you didn't allow dogs in here," Quentin says in the hopes that he isn't hallucinating.

"Hell no, ain't no dogs in here! Well, I guess Petey does come up in here looking for scraps, but ain't much else we can do to keep him from getting where he wants to be. Big fella, eye level at the shoulders and gotta be pushin' seven-hundred pounds."

"Shit!" Quentin is filled with as much curiosity as panic at the new information. "I forgot this was bear country."

"Bears?" The shopkeeper pauses to scratch his head. "Well, bears it is then, I suppose."

Quentin stares at the shopkeeper blankly as he grabs his change. "Thanks for the beer."

"Not a problem, stranger. Enjoy your weekend. Oh, and keep an eye on the subfloor heating while you're up there. Critters love climbing up in there, the rest of us switched to central heat a decade or so ago."

Quentin feigns a smile as he lifts his bags and walks outside. He sees Tina petting Sadie intently as he approaches. The pair give each other a wide-eyed stare and nod their heads at the car. The old man is back to chewing on his cigar and muttering to himself.

"Good talking to ya, missy. I don't mean to scare you city folk, but as the self-appointed leader of the neighborhood watch it is my duty to inform you about potential dangers in these parts."

"Thanks, Cleatus," says an aggravated Quentin walking to the car.

"Name's Marshall, but I'll let that slide. One last thing before you go, there's a saying we have up in these parts. Might be something for the lady to keep in mind. It goes a little somethin' like this:

When mountain towers,
And danger glowers,
Ask the flowers,
To grant you powers.
When the night,
Absorbs the light,
Receive your might,
And aid the fight.
Embrace the change,
Endure the pain,
Release your fangs,
Where evil reigns."

Quentin pauses for a second, nods, and climbs in the car. He turns to Tina and says, "Those people are so fucking weird!" Mike is ripped out of his slumber by the noise and lets out an audible shriek.

"Don't fucking scare me like that, dude!" Mike shoves

Quentin as he wipes the sleep away from his eyes. "I just had the weirdest twenty minutes of my life, man."

"Oh, did you? Did you really, Mike? Don't even start with me." Quentin rolls his eyes and pulls the car back onto the road in a hurry.

"Whatever dude, I'm just vibing here," says Mike, unaware of everything the other two passengers just saw and heard.

The car zigs and zags through the forest road in complete silence, a total shift from the party mode they had when they left home. As they approach the cabin, they notice that the bird spikes are much larger than usual and the subfloor areas of the neighboring cabins are boarded up firmly. Some of the cracked and torn boards are patched up with smaller boards or sheet metal.

Their cabin is more rundown than those around it, and the boards over the bottom of the house are almost all broken. The bird spikes are rusted over and hold the flesh of their latest victim in some spots. Under the cover of the slanted carport sits a sleek, black luxury car.

"Looks like we're the last ones here," says Quentin. "Shit, Tracy drives fast."

"She can drive however she wants, man," says Mike with a dreamy smile on his face.

"Oh, come off it, numbnuts!" Tina laughs and rolls her eyes. "You know she's fucking Javier, right?"

"Um, three things," says Mike in a condescending tone. "First, fuck you, figuratively. Second, you don't know that for sure. It could just be a rumor. Third, you're just jealous that you aren't in on the action. I've seen you staring at them, dreaming of what you wanna do to Javier."

"Ummm, right couple, wrong partner," says Tina as she climbs out of the car. "Come on Sadie, let's get you pottied while the boys unload the car."

Mike shoots Quentin a confused glance but notices that his friend isn't looking back at him. They unload the bags and food, then make their way into the cabin.

"We brought beer!" An excited Mike shouts as he kicks open the cabin door. "Lots of snacks, and finer goodies too. I grabbed those cheese sticks you like, Tracy."

Tracy stands in front of the fridge, unable to reach the top shelf if not for the wedge sandals she wore. Her chestnut skin contrasts against the white metal of the fridge, and her shorts are perfectly tailored to show off her most defining feature. Next to her stands Javier, a tall man with golden skin and a short beard with a well-defined edge.

The group gives their hugs and pleasantries, and both Mike and Tina manage a slightly lower-than-necessary hand on the small of Tracy's back. Mike gives Javier an awkward handshake and makes eye contact with two strangers on the couch in the living room. His pause causes Tracy to jump in and speak for her friends.

"Oh, sorry," says Tracy. "These are my work friends, Olivia and Margie. They're fine sleeping out here, I know space is tight and one room is full of old scrap wood like it's a woodshop."

Olivia is a tall woman with curly brown hair and a dangerously short crop top made from an old rock band shirt.

Margie has short dirty blonde hair and a small diamond nose stud that stands out against the posh style of her otherwise conservative work attire.

"Don't mind Mike, we're just shaken up from the drive. I'm sure we'll make it work," says Quentin in a reassuring tone. "I'm due for another joint if anyone wants to join me on the patio."

The group makes their way outside to watch the sunset from the spacious patio. The breeze starts to cool off, and the smell of rain blankets the air. Quentin and Tina share a shrug of acceptance as if to say that the cabin is nicer than they expected after their run-in with the locals. As the sun dips below the horizon, Sadie sits up tall and begins sniffing and whining at something in the woods. Suddenly, a puppy stumbles out of a bush and falls over, like a baby learning to walk.

"It's ok Sadie," says Tina calmly. "It's probably just a neighbor's dog."

"Sadie is such a cute dog, Tina," says Olivia. "How did you find her?"

"She found me, actually," says Tina. "I was walking through a shelter and she just kept howling until I pet her. I like to think she chose me for a reason I'll never understand."

"So sweet," says Olivia. "She knew you would always take care of her."

As the strange puppy gets closer, Tina and the group realize that this puppy has the proportions and coordination of a small puppy, but is easily fifty pounds. The markings on its fur and the shape of its face make it clear that this is a wolf pup.

"It's so cute! I just want to squeeze it!" Tracy exclaims

between coughs as she rips another hit from the joint.

"No way, babe," says a cool and collected Javier. "That's a wild animal, and if that's a puppy I don't want to see its momma."

"Smart move, Javier," says Olivia. "Also, this rain is coming down hard, we should go close the windows in the house."

"Fine, I'll leave it alone," bemoans a sad Tracy.

As the group heads inside, Mike chats with Olivia, eager that gravity will do something tricky with what's left of her shirt.

"Need a hand with those windows?" He asks sheepishly.

"Go fuck yourself, creep." Olivia stares at him coldly before closing the window near her.

"Hey Mike, I could use a hand in here," yells Margie from the upstairs bathroom.

Mike lets out a low sigh and runs upstairs to help her out. He walks towards the window and sees Margie behind the door with her heels off, blouse unbuttoned, and a finger in her mouth. She grabs him and pushes him against the window while she brings her lips inches from his.

"I hear you're trying to fuck."

"That, that, that could be accurate. Yes," stutters a flustered Mike. "I didn't expect you to be like this, with the fancy clothes and the MILF hair."

"Just shut up, Mike," she says while kissing his neck. She slides her hand down his chest and abdomen, then reaches into his jeans to grab a handful of throbbing bits. She uses her other hand to slide his hand up her thigh and into her pencil skirt. As his hand reaches her panties, she lets out a terrible shriek and points at the window as she falls against the door. Just then, a massive claw reaches through the open screen and digs into Mike's shoulder, leaving a few deep scratches.

Mike falls to the floor in pain just as Quentin barges into the bathroom with a broom and manages to scare off the attacking creature. He closes the window and helps Mike up to his feet while he surveys the damage before noticing the half-naked Margie on the ground.

"Shit, you never catch a break, do you numbnuts," says Quentin with a poorly masked fearful tone in an attempt to lighten the mood. "Get all the windows shut as soon as you can! It was a fucking wolf!"

Margie bolts out of the bathroom, covering herself with her hands, and hides behind a shocked Olivia while she gets dressed. Quentin walks his injured friend downstairs and sits him on the kitchen counter for Tracy, the med school student, to examine. She cuts off his shirt, cleans the scratches, and dresses his wounds with band-aids from her first aid kit. Meanwhile, Mike is too traumatized to process that his childhood crush is spending so much time touching him. Quentin and Margie catch the group up on the encounter, much to their surprise.

"How did it come through the screen?" Tracy asks.

"Fuck that, how did a wolf get on the roof?" Javier interjects.

Sadie begins barking at the patio, and Tina attempts to comfort her. Quentin approaches the window slowly and notices three wolves walking out of the bushes, all far larger than

Sadie the large shepherd. He turns to tell the group as a series of loud bangs erupt from the other side of the house. The group pauses in fear. Scurrying and whining noises come from the floorboards below.

"The subfloor heating!" Exclaims Quentin. "That old fucker at the store was right." He turns the heater on full blast and a loud whelp is heard followed by frantic banging as two more wolves run out of the subfloor. The people approach the windows to watch the event.

An even larger wolf leaps out of the woods to check on the injured, this one is easily twice Sadie's size.

"Holy shit it's huge!" Shouts Javier. "That has to be the alpha of the pack."

More wolves flood the lawn, two more the size of the giant that Javier wrongly assumed to be the pack leader, for a total of thirty hungry wolves. Tina remembers the poem spoken by the old man outside the store, slowly piecing together that he knew far more than he led on.

"We should board up the windows with the wood from that one room," says Javier after regaining his composure. "Margie, can you and Olivia take Mike upstairs?"

Javier and Quentin start feverishly nailing boards to the walls, finally noticing all the old nail holes from previous tenants in the same situation. Tracy helps the assembly line by picking up nails and boards to bring to the makeshift carpenters. Tina brings Sadie upstairs and notices the bent bird spikes where the previous wolf made it on the roof. She climbs out the small window and fiddles with the spikes in hopes of bending them back.

The carpenters finish barricading the downstairs and regroup with the rest upstairs to watch Tina fix the spikes. The world goes silent for Tina as she fixes the last spike, with no sound of rain hitting the roof, or of her friends who she can see shouting at her. The only feeling she has is the hot breath on her shoulder as she turns to see a massive wolf climb on the roof with no concern for the spikes she risked her life to fix. Taller than Javier, this growling beast must be hundreds of pounds but has the mobility of a house cat. He sniffs the air around her and pulls back for a split second. She crawls away as fast as she can and barely escapes the jaws of the monster.

The group stands in shock as they stare down an utter monstrosity outside the window.

"That must be fucking Petey," says Quentin. "The motherfucker from the shop knew this was up here and he didn't tell us! We gotta barricade the upstairs now, too."

The group makes quick work of the remaining windows and locks themselves in a large room facing the balcony. The door is barricaded with two layers of thick wood and all the remaining nails they could find. The group can hear the smaller wolves scratching at the door, but the barricade doesn't give an inch.

Sadie sits in front of Tina and starts howling, the same way she does at home to get Tina to play with her.

"Not now sweetie, please don't antagonize them," says a terrified Tina. "We'll play later, I promise."

Sadie howls louder and paws at Tina's hands aggressively.

"Fuck it," says Quentin. "I'm high as hell and they're already angry."

Quentin begins to howl, and other humans join in. Tina joins in the howling as well but makes a noise more like a wolf howling than a human mimicking a wolf. The scratching at the door stops as the smaller wolves scurry away. A loud thud shakes the entire exterior wall and a second shatters the whole barricade, leaving the group face to face with a hungry wolf larger than a horse.

The group stops howling and backs up against the wall, all except for Tina who has gone from a howl to a deep growl. Petey charges at her, but not before she instinctively lunges at him to protect Sadie and her friends. Her muscles feel like they're on fire, probably from adrenaline she assumes. She feels an urge to sink her teeth into her opponent, teeth that feel longer and sharper than they should be. She feels herself overpower the massive beast and gives into her urge to bite and tear and shred. Tina digs into the throat of the wolf, eventually tearing off its head.

She tries to grab the head to throw it away from her, but can't seem to use her hands properly. A quick glance shows that her hands have turned into massive paws, so she picks up the head with her teeth and carries it over to the balcony. A complete change in physiology should be a shock to Tina, but somehow it just feels right. It feels like freedom.

The smaller wolves outside have fled to the edge of the forest and she jumps down to the ground below with ease, thanks to her new canine physique. She drops the wolf's head near the other large wolves who lick her wounds as a sign of submission to their new leader.

Sadie makes her way downstairs to join her owner, and Tina ensures that she is accepted into the pack. Tina, Sadie, and their new pack disappear into the woods, leaving their human friends with an unbelievable story and a wrecked cabin.

"What the fuck was that?" Asks Mike, voicing the concern of the whole group.

The group members pack up their belongings and run out of the cabin as fast as they can. Margie volunteers to tend to Mike's wounds on the way to the hospital, following Tracy's instructions. Quentin and the others try to come up with a reasonable explanation for Tina's disappearance.

Lemonberry

It's a sad soul that knows joy without grief,
For the sour of the lemon makes the strawberry taste sweet.

My Heart Hurts

In a kitchen with sand-colored tile and glossy white cabinets, a man stands in front of a silver french door refrigerator. He hides his head from the morning light reflecting off every corner of the ivory box around him while trying to find something that sounds even remotely appetizing. The man's charcoal lounge wear absorbs all the light around him, leaving a dark blob that is a fitting metaphor for his current state.

"Where is the ice cream?!" The outburst is so unexpected that it confuses him and catches him off guard, but then the anger brings a sense of comfort and control, so he leans into it. "WHERE IS THE ICE CREAM?!"

He throws his arms to the side as he shouts, knocking the water pitcher out of the fridge. The man doesn't even notice the pitcher as it falls to the floor, not until it bursts open and sprays water across the whole room.

"FUCK!!" The words ring out with as much pain as anger. He slams the fridge doors closed and turns around, leaning his back against the fridge.

As he groans and puts his hands over his face, he notices a blueish-white spectral figure in the puddle of water. The man pauses for a second, unwilling to investigate further. He overcomes his fear and moves his hands away from his face to look at the figure standing in front of him. The ghostly figure is a young boy, around six years old, dragging a fuzzy rainbow-colored stuffed animal behind him. The man lets out an audible cry and then slides to the ground sobbing uncontrollably.

"Hi Dad," says the little boy. "I'm better now, no more needles or machines. I'm free and I can dance again. See?" He lets out a little twirl to show off his dance moves.

"I'm with grandma and grandpa now. We play chess and read old books together. Grandpa says he has a cold one ready for you, whatever that is, and not to rush over kiddo."

"I miss you, son, it hurts so bad," says the father, clutching his heart.

"I know Dad. Your heart stores all your love for me and now it has to make room for my love for you. That's why it hurts. I'll be ok now, I promise."

"Don't leave me again."

The boy puts his hands over his dad's hands as he fades away slowly.

As the man sits crying on the floor, a woman comes in and places bags on the counter. She drops to her knees and comforts her husband.

"I'm here with you," she says.

"Are you here to get me off the ground and cheer me up?" He asks in a snarky tone.

"No," she says calmly. "My support means I'll be on the floor as long as you are. I miss him too."

"I know you do," he says with resignation.

"Look, I bought more ice cream. I finished ours last night."

My Heart Hurts

She grabs the carton from the counter and hands it to him eagerly, with a smile on her face.

The man cracks a pained smile as he takes the ice cream from her.

Dedicated to Dunny Bunny and anyone who lost a child, human or pet. I love you, Libby.

Book Three

The Future

A look at how it shall be.
A collection of worlds filled with endless possibilities,
science fiction made fact, and the spread of humanity
through the cosmos.

The Bar Dive

A woman, Denise, sits alone in a floating restaurant orbiting a red giant star from the outer edges of its developing solar system. Her white satin dress brilliantly reflects the view of the stars seen through the window behind her, and contrasts against her amber brown skin and dark curly hair pulled up into an elegant top bun. Denise is anxiously waiting for someone while trying to seem composed. She looks around the room and rubs her temple with her right hand.

She inspects all corners of the room, the round pedestal tables shared between the leather lounge chairs, all beneath hanging pendant lamps to complete the vibe of a mid-twentieth-century club on a planet far from here. The patrons decorate the furniture with their array of clothing styles, skin tones, and various forms of dining etiquette. The warm glow of the vintage lamps carve out shapes stolen from the cool glow of the celestial backdrop. Most important to her are the eyes returning her glances and the location of exits—one is the entrance she used, and the other an emergency airlock just past the bathroom.

A man approaches and places his leather messenger bag on the table. He is tall and slender with seashell white skin and short dirty blonde hair sporting a side part. A black and white suit finishes off his appearance as a run-of-the-mill corporate worker who just escaped a meeting to make it on time.

"The stars burn ever so bright tonight," he says.

A code, it's him. Her buyers are usually men to keep up the impression of a date. Even in a world with interstellar travel two women on a date attract attention, all of which is unwanted. Men really can harness the power of quantum entanglement for instant pizza delivery but still can't understand why a woman doesn't want to be interrupted at dinner.

"Indeed they do. I prefer the solar eclipses, so beautiful in a binary star system like this." She says begrudgingly.

She never liked codes with bad astronomical data in them, the nearest binary system is three light-years away.

"You should see the blue sunrise. It's beyond belief."

Beyond belief is true, as the myth was debunked thirty years before. Proven to be a hoax put on by a neighboring galaxy to increase tourism, an impressive feat even though it distracted half the field of astronomy for a decade. Blue stars do exist, of course, but not ones that change color on a frequency entrained with the working hours of tourist outposts. Unfortunately, the bad information remains as secret codes are more important than facts to many buyers.

"Do you have many friends in this star system?" She asks, continuing with the older code he is using.

"Not so many near me," he responds.

"None here with me," she thinks to herself.

That's the correct response, words are important here. Why use the old code only to mess it up? Is it a translation issue with the linguistic cipher or merely a misremembering during a nervous moment? Could this be related to the rumblings she'd heard of corporate spies who managed to steal an old form of the cipher? Was it *this* form of the cipher?

The tick again. Hand to the temple in a rubbing motion to trigger her optical implant. She quickly scans the room looking for a reddish glow. She spots two at the bar in baggy suits to hide their fusion blasters. Nasty things, exploding at the quantum level to kill you before you even catch up to that point in time. Death from the future, they're called. Two more at a table opposite the bar, near the entrance. Alas, even the buyer himself glows. He is covered in oxidized uranium sulfate powder from a neighboring galactic volcano, likely the corporate base in the Canis Major Dwarf Galaxy.

"Credit is given where credit is due," she says to make sure he brought payment.

A few fingers tap on the bulging pocket in the front of the designer bag to imply the presence of untraceable credits from multiple galactic exchanges. But, even with the label intentionally scratched away by a few well-placed wear and tear marks, the color and pattern of the stitching are an obvious tell that the bag is from Wolfhyde Leatherworks in that same CMD galaxy. A setup!

"Perfect, the data disk is hidden in the ladies' room. I'll be back in a moment," she says as she moves slowly towards the bathroom.

A few taps on her watch disguised as a nervous tick and she signals for a ride-share to pick her up thirty thousand miles away, between her and the nearby sun. Gravity plunges are very dangerous, but so is being imprisoned for treason against a corporation. The massive star has enough gravity to pull her directly into its molten core, immediately disintegrating her. It also has enough pull to take her away from this restaurant in a hurry like a rock from a slingshot. Her aim has to be absolutely perfect.

The two bar goons stand up to follow her as she rounds the corner, thinking she can't see them through the plant wall. Years of espionage teach one how to see without being seen, reflections on steel tables and picture frames can be more valuable than mirrors or cameras.

She quickens her pace down the hall and reaches her hand into her purse to pull out a viscous iridescent liquid that begins to crawl up her arm, over her cocktail dress, and down to her opera heels. The transparent layer forms an airtight seal and shimmers as brilliantly as the vast cosmos outside. She flicks a plastic bag out to open it as it hardens into a clear glass-like dome almost immediately before joining with the liquid bodysuit. Hard to believe space suits used to be so clunky and hard to assemble.

She pulls the emergency alarm, jumps into the airlock, and waves at the two goons who stop in their tracks as they see the outer doors begin to open. No space suits it seems, bummer. A high-speed chase through an asteroid field is always better on foot, spaceships are just too clunky. The airlock sequence completes and the outer doors open to grant her access to the cold vacuum of space. Without the anti-gravity shield provided by the restaurant the massive sun begins to pull on her immediately, so she braces herself against the wall and railing. She holds her watch arm out in front of her body at a right angle and grabs the elbow of the arm holding the railing to form a stable pose for navigation. She rotates her body left and right until the watch glows green at the top to signal she is aimed directly at the target—a few arcseconds of error will turn into miles at this speed. Not to mention the complexity of recalculating orbital dynamics on the fly.

Liftoff.

As she leaves the manufactured gravity of the restaurant she feels herself go into freefall accelerating towards the star. She lets herself dive into the gravity of the massive red giant with enough rocket fuel for a few minor corrections and a fusion blaster with two rounds—women's fashion doesn't leave much room for storage. The orbiting restaurant is cruising at twenty thousand miles per hour and her speed increases rapidly from there due to the intense gravitational pull of the star. She barely dodges an asteroid hurtling towards her as she notices another directly in her path. A direct hit from her blaster and the asteroid implodes into a tiny neutron star which slightly alters her flight path. One round left and halfway to her destination.

Ten minutes of constant acceleration sends Denise careering at twenty miles per second, yet the infinite cosmos around her feels motionless and silent. With no wind to push on her helmet, she would have thought she was floating in place save for the speedometer on her watch. The myriad of colors from the waterfalls of nascent stars shine ancient light on her helmet, light emitted millennia ago on a mission to reach her eyes at this very moment. The duality of watching the birth of stars that may have already collapsed into black holes is an easy distraction. No time to watch in awe, death can come without notice in the wastelands of space.

Her destination slowly becomes visible, so she gently alters course and slows her approach to soften the landing. Even a small pebble at her current velocity could tear through a warship. She is finally able to break her navigation pose and taps her watch to alert the driver of her approach. The doors open on her side and the driver sends out an antigravity shield to help her land with ease. The craft isn't much larger than a twenty-first-century sedan and the doors are slightly smaller than a human standing upright—not much different than landing a parachute on a jet ski in the middle of the ocean. Denise uses the last of her rocket fuel to slow to a float and lands gently in the backseat.

"For Denise?" She asks the driver. "Apologies for the rough landing."

"Yes ma'am. Even the roughest of landings are softened by the presence of friends," he replies.

"Indeed they are," she says with a smile. Finally, someone got the code right.

"To Alpha Centauri, your lordship?" He asks.

"Nebulas, no," she retorts while fixing her makeup and staring at her compact. "The cyber disco clubs in Orion's Belt. I look too good to go back to the office."

"You got it," he says.

The ship collapses the antigravity shield and uses the

gravitational pull of the sun to gain speed. A wormhole opens in front of them and they escape to the dive bars located on the perpetually dark side of a planet orbiting the star Alnilam.

Maybe the next deal will bear better fortune.

Reverbs vs Juicers

At the crossroads of a dozen major galactic trade routes, fifteen thousand lightyears along Meersh's Voyage, lies a small planet covered in lifeless deserts and decrepit cities yearning to house the occasional traveling merchant. The planet shelters a few thousand traders at a time, yet the hotels have the capacity for a million times that many. The hotels are maintained as much as possible, but the tallest of the towers lean a bit starting at around the two hundredth floor. A mechanical forest made up of gnarled steel trees built hundreds of years ago.

The planet would seem an ill fit for the title of "sporting capital of the universe" if not for the utter behemoth of a stadium on the edge of the city. The massive dome-shaped stadium is nearly two miles long and over a thousand feet high, boasting a capacity of almost thirty million spectators. When all the exterior lights are on, the stadium is called "the planet's second sun" and is capable of making never-ending daylight that stretches hundreds of miles.

For a short period in the planet's orbit, it is contained entirely within the crossroads, making it the perfect place to host the Galactic Cup. The Galactic Cup is a tournament where the best teams of Reverbs and Juicers go head to head in various dangerous and unforgiving games, such as Glitch Ball. Glitch

Reverbs vs Juicers

Ball teams can have a mix of Reverbs and Juicers, but the teams that perform well enough to reach the Galactic Cup tend to favor one style of play.

Reverbs are named for their cybernetic enhancement suits, exoskeletons that charge up using the kinetic energy of the speakers lining the otherwise perfectly polished arena floor. This means they must move with the rhythm of the music being played and have to charge after making extreme plays. Reverbs tend to be light on their feet, using acrobatics and nimble martial arts as an advantage over the slower Juicers.

Juicers, on the other hand, are named for the veritable Brompton Cocktail pumped into their veins which consists of anabolic steroids, ketamine, amphetamines, and state-of-the-art electrolytes. Due to their insanely muscular physiques, they tend to move slower than Reverbs and don't live nearly as long, but the all-star Juicers can go head-to-head with a Reverb any day. Juicers aren't bound to the rhythm of the court and prefer to conserve their energy by avoiding dramatic movements.

Today marks the first day of the games, and the streets are packed. Hover car parking is overbooked and smells of beer and cookouts. All thirty-six public entrances have a six-hour wait time and concessions are sold to those waiting. A private entrance sits at the top of the stadium and is surrounded by a hover fence covered in signs that read "VIP entrance only, your entrance is on the lower levels".

Classism is prevalent during the season of the games, especially between the wealthier tourists and the locals competing for their disposable income. The planet's main source of income is tied to the Galactic Cup and its peripheral industries. A billion temporary visitors need somewhere to sleep, sometimes someone to sleep with, and something to eat. Millions who can't afford a stadium seat still travel here to watch the game on a quantum holovisor at a nearby bar.

The holovisors are entangled with tracker electrons at the main event, allowing those within a few hundred miles to view the event in all three dimensions just as it happens. Decoherence of the atomic superposition increases with distance, leaving those on the outskirts with a glitchy feed that resembles animated sand art.

Today marks the start of a dream come true for an athlete from a nearby star system, a young man named Netim. He's been picked for an all-star team of Reverbs! His taxi takes him around to the athlete's entrance far from the busier general entrances, all while Netim is nervously rambling nonstop.

"Wow! The stadium is huge! So much different than playing in the streets back home. You from here originally?"

"No," says the driver in a curt but unannoyed tone. "Just came over to drive for a few days. It's quick cash and I avoid the nighttime drunk crowds after the games. How long have you been training with this team?"

"Oh, today's the first day. I heard my star system's team had a spot open and put in an application. I got accepted so I'm here to train. I'm gonna be the Cup champion one day. Hopefully, I get to watch the game too, I'd love to check out what a crowd this size is like."

"Uh, training season is over, kid. Are you sure you're not

here to play? Wouldn't be the first time they've thrown fresh meat into the ring."

"No way! They would have told me. Right?"

The driver taps his fingers on the steering wheel while sighing and letting out an amused grin.

"Well, we're here at the entrance," says the driver while pulling up to the door. Netim climbs out and walks away as the weight of uncertainty and nervousness comes over him for the first time.

"Netim!" shouts the driver as he begins to drive off. "Good luck out there, I believe in you."

An angry crossing guard blows their whistle at the driver, who looks at them and shrugs. "Cool it! I'm amping up the next Cup Champion here!"

He drives off quickly and an attendant walks up to Netim to check his papers.

"Right this way, Netim. Your Cup Championship awaits you," says the attendant with a subtle sense of sarcasm as he points towards the locker rooms.

Netim follows the attendant through long hallways and various storage rooms until he finds his team's locker room. He finds them all sitting in their Reverb suits looking game ready. Mostly men but a few women, with a variety of body types among them. Female suits show a feminine physique but don't draw attention to it and are as functional as the mens' suits, just like the players.

Netim's new teammates stare back at him, some waiting for him to take their lunch orders and others with more friendly looks. One of the people not in uniform gestures to an open locker at the end of the row that has his name on the door. His name is written on a piece of tape sitting overtop of a dozen other pieces of tape, a dark homage to his predecessors.

"Last more than a game and I'll make you a plaque by hand, newbie. I'm sure they got the stains out of your suit though," boasts a skinny man with a well-manicured beard who shoves Netim into his locker with a chuckle. A few of the teammates join in, but another near the man elbows him back as a signal to take it easy on the new kid.

Inside the locker is a full Reverb suit and helmet! Totally articulated movement powered by next-generation nanotechnology and myoelectric command systems. Netim is hit with another wave of nervousness as he realizes just how far he is from the streetball he's used to. He shakes it off and begins to learn how the suit functions.

"I'm not here for training, am I?" A rhetorical question from Netim.

"No, you're a full team member as of today, Netim."

The man speaking is older than Netim, likely in his forties based on the salt and pepper color of his hair and the gravel in his voice. His forehead has some wrinkles to it and a large scar, likely from an accident during a game of Glitch Ball. His eyes are kind but focused on the wall as he thinks about how to lead the team through today's game.

"I'm surprised you let me play with so little training."

"We've had... trouble... keeping two of our slots filled. All the trainees who finished training are old news."

Reverbs vs Juicers

The man finishes his sentence and looks away to end the conversation and get back to his preparation. A bell rings in the locker room and half of the team walks down the hall where they will wait to be dropped into the court to start the match.

Netim and the other backup teammates watch the game through a large window looking out over the crowd. Bright neon lights flash all around the court, both from illuminated players and from the audio-driven lights in the court itself. The size of the crowd, and the seismic activity from it, is astounding. A loud siren erupts and the teammates waiting in the hall are dropped straight into the court opposite a group of large, burly Juicers.

Loud electronic music begins playing and a strange-looking ball shoots out from the middle of the court. One of the Reverbs rockets ahead to catch the jump ball. The player beats the Juicer to the ball, but is hit with a right hook from the slower opponent. The Reverb spins wildly and bounces on the court, but maintains control of the ball.

"Nice! They won the jump!" Shouts an excited Netim.

Netim eagerly watches the match, learning the rules added for the Galactic Cup and getting a feel for the massive court. Both teams deliver massive blows against their opponents in an attempt to steal the ball.

One particularly large Juicer catches a Reverb right in the face with a nasty blow. Their helmet shatters and they collapse to the floor immediately. The loud siren erupts again and the other players are frozen in place by large magnets. The tile holding the downed teammate begins to lower to allow for medical staff to attempt a resuscitation.

"Oh man, his suit is just leaking everywhere!"

"That ain't the suit, kid," says the coach.

"That dude just died?!!" Netim's scream echoes with shock and bewilderment.

"I'm watching."

"People can just die in this game?!"

"Why do you think there was a spot open? You're on, ball out."

Netim is dropped from the box down into the court to take the place of the recently removed teammate. He soaks in the roar of the crowd and their bloodlust, the flash of the lights, and the silence between the hits of the woofers.

The interior of the stadium has three sections. The lower section is full of drunk and screaming fans waiting for an accident to happen. The middle has slightly more elevated fans who are better at hiding their morbid fascination. The upper area is a box floating over the lower sections and encased in one-way glass to preserve the privacy of the guests.

Netim pauses to think about whether he's ready for it and starts to scream from fear.

"Can it man, for fuck's sake. We can hear you," grumbles the skinny bearded man from the locker room.

"This ain't streetball," says the team leader. "If you pick that ball up you take on responsibility for anything that can come your way. I'm tired of being stuck to this wall, so be quick. "

Netim steps forward and grabs the ball with a shaky hand. The music picks back up and the other players drop off the wall. The game becomes a blur to Netim who tries not to ruin the game for the rest of the team.

As the match nears the end, another siren signals the final game mode. The ball glitches away from the players and floats in front of the VIP booth, out of reach. A transparent dome forms around the Juicers and the goal in the middle of their circle. The dome powers down any electronics that enter, leaving Reverbs to play as Normies. One advantage is that Juicers can't score points, but they can easily shred a defenseless Reverb who enters the circle.

Netim eyes the goal and moves into position to charge it. He can catch the ball before it drops and ends the minigame.

"What the hell are you doing, newbie?" Asks the team leader.

"Gotta take the lead, ya know," says Netim.

"That's how we lost the other newbies," chuckles another teammate. "Only one suit has ever made it out of the death dome intact, and it ain't yours."

"To hell with them," says the skinny beardy with obvious malice. "You got this."

"I got this." The words rattle around in Netim's brain until they bump into the memory of the taxi driver from just a few hours before.

"I believe in you. Next Galactic Cup champion."

That settles it, the championship won't win itself and this is why he's here. The ball drops slowly and begins to accelerate towards the sweaty mass of roid rage blocking the goal. Netim fires up his skates and focuses on his years of streetball experience. He can take a beating.

As he crosses through the dome, all electronics in his suit power down immediately. His legs gain back their full weight and his skates become much harder to roll forward. In what feels like slow motion, Netim slides under the legs of a surprised Juicer and grabs the ball just before it touches the ground. He sees a massive arm swing towards him and just manages to dodge it. He then jumps off the knee of his assailant and backflips into the air well above the other Juicers, landing just outside their huddle.

The goal is in sight and he dashes towards it at full speed, speed being the one advantage he still has. He leaps into the air and throws the ball at the goal, but is caught by a solid strike to his side that sends him flying out of the dome. His suit powers up as he slides away and begins to heal his cracked ribs immediately.

"You did it! You crazy bastard," says the team leader with an excitement previously unseen from him. "We're in the lead again! We're on defense now, team. Just keep them from scoring and kick the shit out of them if you have to."

The game continues for a few more minutes and ends with a victory for the Reverbs. The teammates congratulate each other, especially Netim for his daring move in the death dome. The team leader has a quick chat with a league official, one that seems heated, then he returns to the group.

"Go eat and rest up, it seems we have another match today," grumbles the team leader.

"A second match?!! They can't do that with bracket matches!" Shrieks an exhausted Netim.

"It's an exhibition match, apparently we got the attention of someone in the VIP box. Newbie, they can do whatever they want. The crowd holds the crown here. This one's for pride folks."

They retire to their locker room to eat and rest before their second match of the day. Excitement runs through the team, as does a sense of curiosity at the unknown match ahead of them. They're tired, but knowing that the match doesn't affect their ranking has eased some tensions.

The Reverbs make their way back to the court anticipating a team to go up against. However, they're greeted by a single woman in a hot pink crop top and jorts skating backwards on regular roller skates with a lollipop in her mouth. Her hair is a vibrant shade of emerald green, a match to her nonchalant yet piercing eyes, her tall tube socks, and her bold eye shadow. She loops around the court with ease and grace reminiscent of twenty-first-century figure skaters on ice.

Netim thinks she's there as some form of intermission, and tries to go on the court to talk to her. A teammate throws out an arm to stop him suddenly, knocking him off balance.

"Newbie! She *is* the next match," says the team leader.

"Haha alright then. Let's get to it."

"Newbie!" Shouts the leader, now with an annoyed tone. "She's in a Cup match with no team, no suit, no hover skates, no juice, and no fear. Use your brain or we'll send you home in a very leaky box."

Netim freezes in acquiescence while he processes his confusion.

The match starts and the woman handles her own as a Normy with gymnast moves and far more strength than one would expect from her figure. She shoulder-checks one of the larger Reverbs and sends him flying thirty feet without effort and skates off with insane speed to score a goal for herself.

The game mode siren blasts to signal a change in the rules, lawlessness.

"Keep your distance! She's far more dangerous than she looks," yells the leader.

Netim ignores the warning and skates up to her to show off his blinding light move, but crashes into a massive wall of rock pulled up from deep beneath the stadium. He regains his focus to see her skating on top of stone pillars emerging from the ground to speed her up and assist her with even more extreme acrobatics.

"Wait. Earth magick?!! Sorcerers are allowed here?" Asks the newbie in shock.

"Which part of lawlessness escapes you?" Snivels skinny beardy.

"They let gods in?!! Is that Atansha?"

"Naw, kid. Gods are too powerful to face us," says the leader. "This must be a daughter of Atansha. Little hell raisers, all of them. She has weaknesses though, no matter how small. Keep airborne when you have the ball and skate more erratically to avoid those erupting pillars. Ball out."

The Reverbs give it their all but are unable to win against the power of the demigoddess. The woman makes another unnecessary goal just as the game ends and skates off the court without even waiting for the cheers of the crowd. She looks over at Netim and winks, a move that is as erotic as it is intimidating given the current context.

The court is in a state of complete disarray, full of holes, and covered in chunks of dirt. Silently, the dirt mounds crumble and are carried by a breeze towards the holes. Once the earth is all gone, the holes heal themselves to form a perfectly smooth court once again.

The controlled breeze is thanks to Yuudil, General of the Winds, high above in the floating VIP box. He chuckles at the rollerblading hellraiser as she takes a seat next to her mother, Atansha. On the other side of Atansha sits a man in brilliantly shining armor made of iridescent scales and decorated with beautiful foliage. His well-kempt beard almost covers an enchanted amulet hanging on his neck. Next to him is an ancient candle burning with a soft flame that illuminates the whole booth, showing off a multitude of gods and other powerful beings.

The Reverbs make their way to the locker room to unwind from a long day. Netim smiles as he leaves the court, knowing that he's well on his way to becoming the champion he wants to be.

Acknowledgments

Thank you to my family who, through their support and disagreement, formed the views responsible for shaping the world I live in. Their sticks and stones formed the foundation of my existence and their words built a vocabulary of expression I use daily.

Thank you to Wancy for cementing the idea of self publishing in my brain. Thank you to friends who not only showed me a world far different than my own but allowed me to live in theirs while I built one of my own design.

Thank you to J.R.R. Tolkien, Michael Moorcock, J.K. Rowling, and George Lucas (as well as countless others) for creating imaginative fiction that inspired me to write this book. Thank you to Aidan Wachter for his book, "Six Ways" (and to Weecho for showing it to me) which set me on my magickal journey. Thank you to Carl Jung for his work on archetypes, and Caroline Myss for her book "Sacred Contracts" (and to K for showing it to me) which affirmed my belief in my inner storyteller.

About the Author

Garrett S. Broussard, author of Cacophony of Crowns, is a software developer for Animation and Visual Effects, photographer, woodworker, hiker, and whisky lover. He enjoys fantasy and science fiction shows of all kinds and calibers, as well as horror and nature documentaries.

He is fascinated with dogs, occult history, and Carl Jung's work on Archetypes.

9 798218 329341